MW01146891

LIBERATION

Book 2 of The Liberation Trilogy

M. C Ronen

mcronenauthor.com

Also by M. C Ronen

THE SHED

IT WAS IN OUR HANDS

LIBERATION - 2nd edition April 2023

1st edition January 2020

Copyright © 2020 M. C Ronen

All rights reserved.

ISBN-13: 978-1-6896-3930-9

To my mum,

who taught me that I am strong, and could be anything I wished to be, regardless of gender, religion, and language, because that's how it should be.

And who at the age of 78, embraced veganism, and taught me that she was strong, and could be anything she wished to be, regardless of age, comfort, and tradition, because that's how it should be.

CONTENTS

ACKNOWLEDGMENTS

I wish to thank everyone who read my first book, THE SHED, the prequel to LIBERATION. It is hard to push through with a book that is meant to address such profound and prevalent ethical misconduct in our society. Thank you to all who read it, and especially to those who contacted me to express their positive review and excitement. My deep thanks go also to all the retailers who either offered or agreed to sell copies of my book.

To my good friend Sandra Kyle, sincere thanks for helping me with first readings, editing early drafts, and providing sound advice. I am deeply grateful for your time and effort, and for your continued encouragement.

To my dear parents, thank you for your encouragement and support. Thank you to my beloved husband, for putting up with me all these years. We make a very good team. Thank you also for helping me with early edits and for your honest feedback. To my son and daughter, not only do I love you *infinity*, but I am so incredibly proud of you both. I hope this book will, in some small way, help pave the way to a kinder world, as you both deserve. To Phoebe, Carlos and Hermione, guardian-children of other species, thank you for making our lives complete. To Luther, running in the golden fields beyond the rainbow bridge, you are always in my heart my sweet boy.

Last but not least, I wish to thank, from the bottom of my heart, the countless passionate, wonderful people around the world, who spend time and energy fighting speciesism and oppression, carrying the vegan revolution on their shoulders, bringing us a better future and freedom for all. You are all heroes.

AUTHOR'S NOTE

While this book contains some scenes of violence carried out by the activists against their opponents, these are for artistic purposes. The author does not support a violent struggle.

M. C RONEN

PROLOGUE

The lovers were running now. Both breathing very hard, their tall silhouettes cutting through the corn and wheat fields, still holding hands. The woman's face was streaked with black smudges, silent reminders of the fire she set to the dormitory building a few days ago. They could hear the sounds of chaos behind them, intensifying. It was dark yet the air was still unforgivingly warm. Trickles of sweat slid down the side of the woman's face. With her free hand she was struggling to keep her long red hair away from her eyes. The man, broad shouldered, long-legged, handsome looking in his construction overalls, was slightly ahead, but kept looking back at the woman, ensuring she was able to keep up.

The grass fields stretched ahead of them now, strewn with flowers. They both stumbled momentarily, in a split second of hesitation. From here on, they would be completely exposed. Behind them, sounds of fast-moving motor vehicles could be heard. They had no choice, they had to go on and give it their very best effort. This was their only chance.

The man briefly reminisced about the last time, not that long ago, they were both in this very place, making their way towards the large electric fence, far in the distance. It was different back then. Sure, they were both tense and deeply concerned about being followed, but they were excited, elated even, by the knowledge of what they were about to do. They were setting up the woman's eldest daughter's escape from this prison farm. The woman's eldest daughter was a teenager and was about to become a dairy slave herself. Setting the girl free from this place would release the woman from the need to protect her, and finally, she herself could escape with him. He could have easily smuggled his lover out of there many times before, along with their baby daughter. He was an outsider, a contract worker in the farm. He came and went as he wished. But the woman wouldn't leave without first setting her elder daughter free. Now that the girl had escaped, it was too late for him and the woman. The farm managers knew what they were up to. The woman set the farm dormitories on fire to allow her eldest daughter time to escape, and they knew it was her. Her time was up. They were going to send her to the "Freeze works" which everyone knew was just a wishy-washy euphemism for the place where all farm slaves were killed. In the days after the fire, he was making every effort to get to his lover, but she was heavily watched, and their baby girl, the only child the woman had ever conceived willingly, was still kept separately and out of their reach. The woman insisted they must snatch their baby girl first, but the man knew they had no time. It was now or never, as his own life would also be hanging in the balance. It was evening when he grabbed her, against her protests and pleads, begging him to go get their child. They will go back for the child; he told the woman. He knew people that could help. She resisted for a while, but he held her hand and made her run. They ran. Frantically making their way towards the same spot where months before they set up the escape point – a thick and heavy fence cover, which would allow them to climb over the electric fence without being fried to a crisp. But management were not fooled and soon enough they were giving chase. They could hear the motors and the shouts, and they could see the headlights moving behind them, getting closer.

The earth was warm, in shades of deep greens and browns, lit by a shy moon, occasionally peeping though a veil of clouds. The man could see the trees getting close. The fence should be stretched amongst these trees, along the horizon line.

"We're nearly there," he managed to say to his lover, his breath heavy, his voice unsteady.

She didn't respond.

Silently they kept running, panting heavily, each breath becoming a struggle. They were getting very close. He could see the fence. They were nearly there. So close.

"STOP WHERE YOU ARE!"

The order was roared menacingly, amplified by the megaphone the slave-farm manager, in her distinct medicinal white coat, was holding to her mouth. Management were collectively known at the farm as 'White Suits', and were all a distasteful bunch in the man's opinion, but this White Suit woman was the worst of them all. A loud, metallic, ear-splitting shot pierced the air. The White Suit woman fired a gun she was holding, directed at the sky. "STOP OR I WILL SHOOT YOU BOTH!"

The man and the woman stopped abruptly in their tracks. The man could hear a small whimper of anguish escape his lover.

They were standing face-to-face with two sparse and roofless vehicles, their engines still humming like two hungry beasts, each with two White Suits seated up front. Four menacing, ill-meaning guns were now pointed at the man and the woman from both vehicles.

The man looked at the woman. They were still holding hands. Her face glistened with tears and sweat, her breath was quick and shaky. He pressed her hand in his, a little gesture of courage. She looked at him, her eyes soft, full of fear but still so determined. She was still so proud, he thought, and so very beautiful.

The White Suit woman, short-haired and svelte, jumped off one of the vehicles. Her megaphone was left on the seat, but the gun she held firmly in her hand. A White Suit man from the second vehicle joined her. They marched towards the two escapees. They were getting close, their faces cold and stern. Then, quite suddenly, they stopped in their tracks. There was no hesitation before the White Suits pointed their guns.

The man turned his head towards the woman. "Stella?" he whispered.

The woman turned her beautiful face towards him. Even at this dire moment, she looked so bold with her stunning red hair.

"I love you, so much," he said, in as steady a voice as he could muster.

"I love you too, David. Forever."

The guns fired.

Sunny's Present Day: Three Years since Joining DaSLiF

1.

I don't dream about my mother as often as I used to. It's been three years since I escaped the farm, and so much has happened since then. In the beginning she came to me at night, or when I was injured and hallucinating. She was still guiding me, I thought, still watching over me. I knew that she had died, I could sense it in my bones, but only later I found out exactly how. She was shot, together with her lover David.

These days my nights are more likely to be ruled by nightmares. Revisited by the ghosts of all I've seen since I climbed the electric fence. After escaping the farm with Spirit, my courageous young sidekick, we were twice rescued. Once by terrible people who really only wanted to enslave us further for their own purposes and greed, and then by a kind couple, a nurse and a doctor, who, by risking their own lives, took care of us like we were their own daughters. They offered us comfort, love and family, and Spirit welcomed it with open arms. As for myself, I chose a different path. I joined the Dairy Slaves Liberation Front (DaSLiF), an activist group that was doing whatever necessary to bring a total liberation to all forms of slavery. In the beginning, I thought there were only dairy slaves, but now I know slavery knows no boundaries. I have seen with my very eyes the horrors of the most bizarre forms of slavery. I know now that, if someone can make a profit out of something, anything, you can bet that somewhere, there is a place where this very thing is being produced - through the brutal exploitation of unwilling others.

I've looked into the heart of evil and the eyes that looked back at me, silent and pleading, hands reaching, begging me to help them, would not let go of me. All the victims, their hands stretched out, reaching out as far as they can reach, grabbing me with surprising strength, reaching, grabbing, begging, holding me in place so tight that I can't escape them, I can't run, slowly I am choked by those I came to free, until I wake in a pool of my own sweat.

We set out to liberate them all, but there are so many of them, and the battle for total liberation is still far from over. I sometimes sink into desperate self-doubting, wondering if we'll ever truly win. I know that we'll never stop until we do. All of us here, all the activists. But how long? How long before it happens?

I can't escape these thoughts as I stride the pale corridors of the bunker towards the large Board Room. Today is the day we are finalizing our preparations for our next big action. This is the action I have been waiting for. We are going to raid one of Natures Farms. One of the main ones. It's "organic" and "sustainable" and all the feel-good words that mean nothing when it comes to herding slaves, raping them, stealing their young and killing them at will. It is the farm where I was born. Where my sister Hope is buried and my other sister, Antim, still lives, as far as I know. It's where my friends were raped in front of my eyes. Where my best friend Rosichi chose death over living with the rape-child she was bearing and didn't want. It's where my mother was shot dead. And here I am, a little breathless, entering the brightly lit Board Room, and the first person to greet me is that same person who held the gun. The woman who killed my mother.

2.

"Sunny!" she says to me with some enthusiasm. Her voice is light, her smile wide. Her teeth are exceptionally white, encased behind very pink, thin lips. Not quite as gaunt as the first time I saw her more than three years ago, her dark hair is shoulder length now, parted in the middle, her tidy fringe neatly cropped. When she was a manager at the farm, she wore her hair short and always parted to one side. This new hairstyle makes her seem softer somehow. Her eyes are slightly narrow, carefully rimmed with black eyeliner and black mascara. A faint, fine web of crow feet wrinkles spreads to the side of each eye as she smiles at me. She still gives me the heebie-jeebies.

"Roth," I reply and nod my head at her. I can't bring myself to smile, but I manage to look a tad less gloomy. At least I hope that's what I'm doing. Maybe I should be kinder to her. A lot has happened since she tried so desperately to capture me. It's been a long while, and still I can't even bring myself to call her Jacqueline. It's too familiar, too personal. I call her Roth.

"This is it then," she says, in what sounds like excitement, still smiling widely, "the one we've been waiting for!"

The one I've been waiting for, I correct her in my head.

"Yup," I say bluntly.

"Back to Natures."

"Yup."

"To your sister."

I look at her intently. Why did she bring Antim into the conversation? Is she trying to unnerve me? To make me emotional? Is she judging me? Measuring me?

I nod.

I don't know how to make small talk with her. I don't want to make small talk with her. Where is everyone?

A sudden commotion in the corridor indicates the meeting is about to start, as a stampede of jovial activists bursts into the room.

"There you are!" A handsome young man walks towards me, his eyes warm and his smile genuine. His ash blond hair a little scruffy, his cheeks slightly red. He approaches me with long, deliberate strides and cups my face in his warm hands as he kisses me lightly on the tip of my nose. "I've been looking everywhere for you, where have you been?"

"Get a room, I'm about to puke!" Pearl shouts at us, her revolted expression deliberately exaggerated.

I can't help but giggle at her. Pearl is a close friend of mine, and I know she is poking fun without a shred of menace. I release myself from his hold. I admit that these public displays of affection still make me feel slightly uncomfortable.

"We already have a room," Ben throws at her nonchalantly. I smile at him. I don't want him to think I resent his hugs and kisses. It's a work in progress for me. *I'm* a work in progress.

"Ech, you two are gross," Pearl says teasingly, her beautiful dark eyes twinkling. She turns to Roth and asks in her singsong voice, "what's up, Jacqueline?" not really looking for a reply as she takes the seat next to her.

I look at them, sitting side by side, opposite me. The ex-dairy slave and the ex-dairy slave owner. Three years, and it's still surreal. Yet Pearl behaves like it's completely normal. It's true that Pearl wasn't a dairy slave for long enough. She was a child when DaSLiF raided our farm and rescued her and a few others. She didn't quite reach the age where abuse and fear became part and parcel of our enslavement. Maybe she doesn't quite carry the same baggage I do. Maybe that's why she is so ready to accept the new Jacqueline Roth, the activist-loving Roth. And I wonder, how come I can't treat Roth with more compassion, when at the same time, *she* could treat Pearl with what seems like genuine kindness. Pearl. The activists who nearly killed her. How come Roth is capable of forgiveness and I am struggling with it?

The noise in the room intensifies gradually, as more and more activists walk in and take their seat by the large board table. I take great comfort in these people. There's a wide representation of people here. We are of varied ages, backgrounds, experience, and appearance. Each one with their own story to tell, what brought them here, what drives them, who they're doing it for?

Everyone greets each other enthusiastically, talking loudly with each other, over each other, darting jokes across the table at one another. *Are they quite as nervous as I am?* I wonder.

Ben reaches for my hand under the table. His eyes are warm and full of reassurance.

"The big one" he says to me, in almost a whisper.

I can't really speak. My stomach churns. I am excited, and I'm nervous, and I'm confident, and I'm scared. I'm so scared. We're going back to Natures. *Natures...* In my mind I recall the billboards advertising Natures dairy product. Happy looking people, real people, not slaves, families... fathers and sons, mothers and daughters, laughing, carelessly holding glasses of white breast milk, enjoying themselves. 'Natures. The REAL taste' the billboards say... *The real taste...*

Finally, an athletic, confident woman walks into the board room, filling it with a lovely scent of flowery shampoo, and the room falls into immediate silence.

Violet is the unspoken leader of our DaSLiF cell. No one formally appointed her to be our leader, but she exudes the kind of natural charisma and drive, that people automatically look to her for direction, motivation, advice, and yes even orders. She does it with not a shred of power lust, but rather matter of factly, as one who strives to accomplish something enormous, with her entire self-bound to that goal. We follow her because we are all here to achieve that goal. Total liberation. Nothing less will do.

I know now that DaSLiF is a ginormous organisation that stretches over huge territories and even across oceans. Two visiting members from another cell are here with us, helping to set up our mission to take down Natures. Their cell, somewhere down south, has managed to put an end to a couple of smaller farms managed by

Natures, only a few months before. There are other leaders under the DaSLiF umbrella, with new cells sprouting into existence almost daily. There is a sense that the ground is quaking underfoot with an all-powerful need for action, in no small measure due to past successes of our own cell. The stories of our actions have travelled like wildfire, becoming almost mythological. And with each success, Violet's persona in the eyes of people has become larger than life. No matter how vehemently she resents this self-glorification, and she does, her very humility is what makes her even more admirable and further glorified. A vicious circle, no doubt.

Violet scans the room with her quick, piercing eyes. As she meets my stare, she holds her gaze. She looks at me as if she is trying to register my state of mind. I can almost believe she can read minds. Finally, she nods.

"Ok, everyone, thanks for coming," she says. Then with a faint smile she looks directly at a young man, sitting at the far end of the room. "Nice of you to make it on time for a change, Nathan."

Nathan smirks "And I even shaved!"

The room erupts into giggles and snorts. The nervous pre-action tension has burst. After all the laughs die down, a more relaxed feeling sets in.

"We spent a long-time planning this," Violet continues. "And D-Day is in forty-eight hours". She pauses and looks around the room. "Is everyone clear with what their assigned tasks are and their exact team allocations? There is no room for error." Everyone nods.

Violet presses a few buttons on the wall, and like magic, a large sky image of 'my' prison-farm is displayed through thin air. I have seen it many times before, as we've been planning our takeover for weeks, yet each time the image appears, seeing it so clearly, so... benignly, makes it hard for me to breathe for a second or two. With my eyes I trace the babies' and toddlers' dorms, where my sister Antim was kept at the time I broke free. I can see the girls' dorms, where she is kept now, most likely, and where I shared so many memories with my best friend Rosichi, who died just before we made it out. Thinking of Rosichi makes my heart sink heavily. Not being able to save her was the biggest regret of my life. Not my only failure to date, but probably the biggest. Behind the girls' dorms, a new building stands, its roof still lacking all signs of degradation and the sort of layered filth that occurs as time goes by. Mocking in its brightness, it stands there, as erect as a middle finger. It's a new women dormitory, to replace the old one that my mother burned to the ground to create the distraction that allowed me time to escape. The ashen remains of the old building are still there, staring accusingly at me. Next are the community hall and kitchen, and past them, the makeshift graveyard. I used to know every single stone and boulder, but now there seem to be more of them. I wonder who has died since I left. I beg Mercy that Antim is not one of those stones. Farther away still, an imposing large building casts a long and heavy shadow. Just looking at it makes the hair on my skin stand on end. This is the building where evil thrives, The Shed. It's where girls are raped, where male babies are kept in jars, and where drugged women are forcefully connected to machines that suck out their breastmilk, together with every shred of their dignity. Natures, the REAL taste. The real taste of death, abuse, and humiliation.

The farm is so enormous that even in the sky image, taken from high above ground, it is almost impossible to trace its borders exactly. In fact, at the north end, the image cuts just under where the farm's boundary is menacingly marked by the slim line of an electric fence.

Violet picks up a purple marker in her hand.

"We'll run it one last time," she says. "I'll point with my marker on the map, and I want to hear from you who's positioned there and what your missions are. Clear?"

Everyone nods. We've been through this before.

"I'll start," Violet says in a firm tone. "So, firstly, we await the signal from our trusted internal contact, nicknamed Golf. Golf will disable the electric fence. Everything kicks off at that point."

We all nod. Golf has been "installed" within Natures the way David was before him. A mole, operating under the guise of being a construction man. None but a select few know Golf's true identity. Some lessons have been learned from when David fell for my mum and was eventually killed.

Violet's purple marker hits at the far end of the image. "North Fence. Shoot."

A white-haired man with a kind face decorated with short white beard responds, "Bill, George, Suli, Simon and Phoenix".

"Thanks Bill," Violet replies. "Your mission?"

"Bombing the fence, disarming any White Suits, raiding the girls' dorms" he says, excitedly.

14

Violet nods. Her hand moves to another point on the map. "Main Electric gate. Shoot."

A beautiful, olive-skinned young woman pushes her beautiful, dark, long hair backwards, as she stretches in her seat. "Leah, Andy, Joshua, Romesh, Suzy, and Alice. Our mission," she continues without waiting for Violet to ask, "is bombing the gate, disarming any White Suits, raiding the womens' dorms". She puts her slender hand on her lap, triumphantly, wiggling her shoulders ever so slightly, like a little dance of accomplishment.

Violet nods. Her hand glides to another point on the fence.

"Fields outside the farm, 500 meters away from gate. Shoot."

"Miley, Bryan, Alicia and Jessica, with a volunteer force of about 150 enthusiasts," says a bouncy young woman, her eyes large and very blue, her voice a little husky.

Violet says nothing, waiting for the young woman to continue.

"We are the key raid force," the young woman continues, her voice like melted chocolate, "our mission is storming through the bombed gates, raiding any and all dorms where help is needed, babies, girls, women, the community hall and kitchen".

"Thank you, Miley," Violet replies.

Now her hand points to a point on the map that I never thought I'd ever see again, in real life, and out of my own free will.

"Side gate, south of The Shed," she says, and I think I detect a slight pause before she looks at me.

15

I clear my voice of the clogged fear that has set up space in my throat. Subconsciously, my finger reaches towards my neck. I run the tip of my finger back and forth, along the peaks and curves of the little shell that is hanging there from a simple necklace. I tend to do that when I'm nervous.

"Sunny, Ben, Pearl and Nathan" I say, my voice still slightly shaky. "Our mission is bombing the side gate, disarming any White Suits, disabling all motored vehicles, and bombing… The Shed". I sense the palms of my hands becoming quite sweaty as I voice our mission out loud. I'll be going into that building again. The premise of so many of my nightmares.

Ben smiles and nods at me. At least this time he'll be there with me.

"Ok, good job everyone," Violet says unceremoniously, and adds dryly, "Also we have me, Peter, and our visiting friends from the south Carl and Dominique in the Command Room, Ren and Venus are our Eye in the Sky operators, and Alec and Billie are again our trusted medics on site."

Everyone nods.

"All right, so, unless there are any other…" She doesn't manage to complete her sentence when across from me I can see Roth raising her hand hesitantly.

Violet is not impressed. "Jacqueline, what is it?" she asks, her voice slightly irate.

Roth smiles faintly, as she lowers her hand back down. "Uhm, where should I be?" she asks.

"As in previous actions, you will be in the Command Room, with Peter and me," Violet responds, turning off the Sky image from the wall.

Thinking that was the end of that, we all start to get up, but Roth continues, her voice somewhat raised, "I... I... eh, I thought this time, you know... with my past experience and familiarity with the place... that I'll be... eh – on the ground? That I'll be joining the troops this time?"

We all look at her with slight astonishment.

"I'd rather you stay in the Command Room," Violet responds unemotionally.

"But, I – I worked really hard for this," Roth says pleadingly, her eyes wide, "I... it's important to me... It's... it's... it's my... *redemption.*"

Violet looks at her for what seems like a potent, long minute. "Let me think about it," she says finally, closing the meeting.

The last thing I want is Jacqueline Roth back on the farm with us. The thought itself is so troubling, I feel a piercing headache forming between my eyebrows. I've never understood why she was allowed access to our actions and missions in the first place. In the past I questioned Violet repeatedly about that. "She provided us with invaluable information" Violet told me. "Without her, some of our raids could not have come to fruition." I understand that, I really do, but I could never quite get over the shock of having her there, with us. I joined DaSLiF three years ago, after escaping the farm where Jacqueline Roth reigned supreme. It was a fresh start, a new life, new purpose, away from the world of my passive-slave past. But having her there was a constant, continuous collision between my new and old lives. A constant reminder. A whirlpool that threatened to suck me back into The Shed, every time I looked at her face.

First Eight Months

with DaSLiF

3.

It was odd, walking the corridors of the old bunker, where Violet's DaSLiF cell took hold. These were historic military barracks and bunkers, used by our human ancestors for their military purposes in olden days, the days before the catastrophes that wiped almost everything out started, with the burning of the Amazon rainforest. Their ancient lives were still echoed from the walls, on which soldiers of old scratched their names, messages, and some profanities. I've been especially haunted by one such carving, etched onto one of the tunnels leading to the Community Room, where someone scratched 'SITREP SNAFU' with an image of a hanged man, dangling from a long noose. It is signed *Sgt. Morgan P*. Often I wondered how long it was before these humans were gone, and what they were forced to endure beforehand. Some effort has been invested in giving this place, that many of us called home, a lighter feel. Some corridors were repainted in bright colours, others had pictures hanging. It had been eight months since I joined this incredible assortment of brave people, and still I felt odd each time I woke up to find myself in the dim lit, windowless room. Back then, in the beginning, I shared my room with Pearl. She was the messiest person I had ever met, but it didn't really bother me. I really liked her. I was so happy that she was back in my life again, after all the years I was so sure that she was dead.

I came to the bunker the same night I decided to join DaSLiF, leaving the warmth and safety of the beach house where Jonathan and Rose, the loveliest people I've ever known, gave me and Spirit our very first home. Real home. The kind of home we should have known from our very first breath. It wasn't easy for Jonathan and Rose to let me go. They were worried for me. But they didn't try to convince me otherwise. Maybe it was also due to the brutal confusion and mayhem that turned everything upside down that day. Jonathan was put in bed, badly wounded, due to Roth having shot him in her final manic attempt to capture me. It's only thanks to Pearl, who intercepted Jacqueline Roth by shooting her, that Rose wasn't shot dead. But Rose was very emotional and having Jonathan wounded meant that her complete focus was given to helping him. She was a nurse, after all, and he a doctor. They knew how to help themselves. They both looked at me with sad eyes as I told them I was leaving to join DaSLiF. They probably knew that this was coming, that my departure was inevitable. Jonathan gave me a faint, reassuring smile, and Rose nodded, tearing up. "You'll be all right, Sunny" she said. "You'll be in good hands".

But it was Spirit who found it the most difficult to see me go. Funny how at the farm I never gave her the time of day. She was nothing but a nuisance to me there. But ever since our escape, she has become the most important person in my life. She saved me more than once, and her bravery easily outdid mine. This little fighter has become as close to me as a sister, and standing at the door, her warm tears streaming down her cheeks, I felt my heart physically breaking inside my chest.

"Don't go, Sunny," she whimpered as her arms tightened around me. "I need you. I need you to stay!"

"You don't need me, silly," I said in what was an attempt at sounding cheerful, but my cracking voice gave my true feelings away. "You have Rose and Jonathan. They are the best people to be looking after you now. No more running scared."

I stroked her lovely hair gently with my hand. "You are going to have an amazing life here, Spirit".

"Then why don't you stay? Don't you want an amazing life too?" she asked, crestfallen.

I sighed. "I do. But my path is taking me somewhere else. I'm needed as an activist, Spirit. I can help them save more of us. I can save Antim."

"But you might get killed!"

"I'll be all right," I said. *Did I actually believe that?* "Violet and all the other activists will look after me. And I promise you, I won't do anything stupid. I promise".

I kissed her pretty, bright forehead, and gave her another hug, as she loosened her hold and allowed me to go. I forced myself not to look back at her, standing at the front door, her cheeks still glistening from tears. In all the eight moths I've been with DaSLiF at the activists' bunker, I haven't gone back to the beach house. I haven't seen Spirit, and I missed her.

Violet, who is Rose's sister, took me under her wing. The first night at the DaSLiF bunker was a blur of names, faces, instructions and such an information overload that I've suppressed all memory of it. I've been told I hardly spoke, did not touch my dinner, and that by nightfall, I placed myself on the bed as I was, fully dressed, and fell asleep. But late that night I woke from a nightly terror, screaming, waking up half the activists in nearby rooms. Pearl sat by my side and comforted me until I fell back to sleep. I remember nothing.

In the weeks since then the bunker has become my home. Amongst all the many faces, a few have become closer to me than others. There was Pearl, my childhood friend, with her enviably beautiful dark skin and generous smile. There was Nathan, who was a bit of a jokester. His fine dark hair always pointed up, and a constant twinkle in his kind, slanted eyes. And there was Ben. My Ben. Well, he wasn't *my Ben* back then, but we were pretty close from the very start. When I was still a dairy slave at the farm, Ben used to watch over me through the cameras installed in drones that DaSLiF operated to intercept Nature's tracking and follow our whereabouts. He spent hours watching me through the Eye in the Sky. *The Eye in the Sky* - That's how the drones are referred to in the bunker. Back at the farm, we called them Sky Noises. We knew nothing of what these things were or where they came from and why. By the time I was finally safe, Ben felt like he already knew me, but to me he was just another new face. Each time he referred to me in a way that showed familiarity, real familiarity, it freaked me out. But his bashful looks, his scruffy ash blond hair and his gentle manners made it easy for me to come to accept his attention.

There was a lot I had to learn. Starting with the communal bunker life, kitchen shifts, cleaning shifts, laundry shifts, armoury shifts. Everything was shifted and scheduled and assigned. By the third evening I was placed on post-dinner cleaning duty with Nathan and a few others, but being as new as I was, and still so confused and disoriented, I nearly missed it. It was Nathan's humouristic and good-natured way of 'unconfusing' me and showing what needed to be done that helped us become such good friends.

Aside from learning the ways of the bunker, there was all the heavy-duty stuff I had to learn. Firing a gun, defusing bombs, setting up bombs, using communication devices, one-on-one combat techniques, disarming opponents, field information-gathering in complete stealth, and mustering The Eye in the Sky. I needed to learn it all, and I needed to learn it quickly. No one told me as much, but I knew there were missions in the planning that depended on me becoming an oiled cog in the machine. Trying to muster all that knowledge, such foreign knowledge, in such a short time, often caused me deep frustration. Instead of proving my worth by excelling at everything, I seemed to suck at every step. It was Violet who came and sat next to me, as I was sulking on my bed, after yet another failure to disarm Bill in training.

"What's going on, Sunny? Talk to me sweetheart," she said, her voice soft.

I took a deep, sulking breath. My cheeks were burning with the burden of my own shame.

"I suck. I suck. I suck! Why did you ask me here? I'm such a failure!"

"A failure? What are you a failure at, Sunny?"

"Everything! I'm a failure at everything! I couldn't even disarm Bill today."

Violet smiled. She stretched her arm out wide and pressed it behind my back. "Come here," she said softly. I leaned my head against her shoulder. Her warmth, the faint flowery scent that radiated from her, this maternal familiarity. I needed it. I wanted it. It was so rare in my life. Stella was loving and caring, but she rarely showed me any real closeness. Part of her was always hard and closed off to me. I needed to sink into these soft arms, to immerse myself in this pool of warm kindness. And as I did, tears started rolling down my cheeks. I was such an embarrassment.

"You think anyone else here could disarm their opponents after three weeks?" Violet asked, her cheek leaning against my head. "Or to assemble a bomb from scratch? Or anything else for that matter? You are asking too much of yourself, Sunny. You will be able to do all of that and more, if you give yourself some time."

I straightened myself up to look at her. "So, I'm not the worst ever?"

"Not even close," Violet laughed. "But the fact that you would push yourself to excel in such a short time here, a place so foreign to anything you've known before, after everything you've been through," she petted my hair softly, "it only proves your qualities sweetheart."

"Am I not holding you up, then?" I asked her, slightly relieved.

"From what?"

"From going on missions? I thought I was holding you up, with my incompetence".

At that, Violet laughed heartily. "Oh Sunny, no. You are not holding us up." And after a short silence she paused and said, with more severity. "There is actually something else I'm waiting for. I didn't think I'd show you yet, but you might need to see."

What was it? I was anxious to know.

"Come with me."

Together we paced the web of corridors, walking in stern silence. It occurred to me that I actually knew enough of the bunker by then, to remember all the twists and turns back to my room. It pleased me. We arrived at the Medical Ward. Here, a few doctors and medics were full-time volunteers for DaSLiF. Alec was the main surgeon, and he had a few assistants. The medical ward was divided into several smaller units. There was a fully established and well-equipped surgery facility, as well as first aid and recovery units. Violet marched in through the first aid unit, passing the little cubicles, with empty beds in each. The resemblance of this room's set up to the place inside The Shed, where my friends were tied up and forcefully impregnated, made me shudder. We walked further, until we reached the wide glass window separating the recovery room from the first aid unit. Curtains were drawn shut on our side, maybe for privacy, or maybe to hide the other unit from view.

"Sunny, what you are about to see will surprise you, but please try not to overreact."

She pulled the curtains, and I screamed.

4.

I must have huffed and puffed into the brown paper bag for ten minutes before I could breathe normally again. Violet was crouched next to me, on the floor where I had collapsed so unceremoniously, stroking my back, trying to calm me down.

Finally, after long minutes, I got up and faced what was on the other side of the glass window. Jacqueline Roth, the White Suit woman, was lying in a bed, plugged into all sorts of machinery. Her eyes were shut. Her face was nearly purple.

"Why is she here?"

"Well, we shot her, so it was our responsibility to try and save her. We're not murderers. That's *them*, not us."

"Yes, but why here? You could have kept her somewhere else."

"She poses no risk to you, Sunny. She won't do anything to you. Not anymore."

"But why here? Why?"

"We need her."

"Need her?" this was incomprehensible to me. "For what?"

"Secrets. Information. Inside knowledge. Anything we can get out of her."

"So, she's definitely going to live?" I remember the circle of blood Pearl's shot triggered in this woman's abdomen. How she fell to the floor just as she was about to shoot Rose. She was very dead-looking to me.

"We don't know. She's still not out of danger."

I stared at the sorrowful near-purple face of the near-lifeless body that was laid on the bed on the other side of the window that separated us. As far as I was concerned, this woman was the Devil.

"What makes you think she'd give it to you, the information, the secrets and all that?"

Violet only smiled. "I can be very convincing when I want to be."

I looked at her, not sure if she was serious. "Are you going to torture her?"

Violet shook her head. "No, no, nothing like that."

I suppose the question marks were all over my face, as she carefully added "Leave it to us. We know how to do it. We'll turn her, you'll see."

Turn her. What does that even mean?

I realised that nothing more would be shared with me just then.

"Let's go back." I said, completely deflated.

"Sunny, one more thing, before we go back," Violet added quickly. "We haven't announced her presence here yet. Not many know. Only the few who were at the beach house that night, when Jacqueline Roth was shot, and of course Alec and his crew. So please, try to keep it to yourself, or only discuss it with those people."

I nodded.

Back in the room that I shared with Pearl, I thanked my good luck for being able to talk about it with Pearl. The two of us were chatting long after lights were out.

"Don't worry, Sunny," Pearl said, "They will turn her to our side. I've seen it done before."

"Really?" that genuinely surprised me.

"Sure."

"Who?"

"I can't say. Not allowed."

"Someone who's here? In the bunker?" I tried my best.

"Can't say."

I let it go.

The next morning, I woke early, and with a sudden unquenchable zeal in my gut. I knew somehow that I had turned a corner. From that moment on, I was going to give it my all, and that I was going to excel at everything I learned, because I was not going to allow the Roth woman to destroy me. I survived in spite of her best efforts, so that meant I was better than her, and I was going to get even better.

I got ready in no time, rushed through breakfast, and entered the Control Room for my Eye in The Sky training like a girl possessed. I was going to master this damn thing. *Today.*

"Whoa!" Ben, my Eye in the Sky instructor, was taken aback by my stormy entrance, but he seemed amused, maybe even impressed.

"Sorry. I'm keen to learn as much as possible today," I said, suddenly moved to say more, stammering foolishly, "not that we didn't before, it's just that today I feel ready. *More* ready…"

Hopeless. But his eyes… I could dive into his eyes and swim in them forever. I liked him, perhaps a little too much. I needed to control my emotions a little better.

"Awesome." He smiled. "Let's do it, then."

We spent hours in the Control Room that day. Long hours of flying the drones, collecting data, blocking, and intercepting signals of farms, analysing information, recording, and downloading. We skipped lunch and kept going well into the early hours of the evening. Finally, Ben stretched his back and groaned "Ouch, I have the shape of a chair."

"We can stop now, if you'd like" I said to him. I didn't mind. It was a good day.

"Let's go and grab dinner and come back later tonight," he suggested. "You need to learn to operate night vision on these things."

My heart rejoiced. More Ben time.

At dinner, Pearl and Nathan joined us at our table. We shared plates of vegetables, beans, and rice, filling ourselves with great quality, healthy and delicious food. There was no flesh, or any other unnatural products consumed here. The conversation started as jovial and carefree, slowly moving to more personal topics, as the tone gradually became sombre. I learned that Nathan was orphaned of his parents several years before, while Ben's family disowned him, after his life-philosophy of total liberation moved him to activism and finally to DaSLiF. "My parents are probably two of Natures' most determined supporters" he said sadly. "Sorry, Sunny".

On a whim, I reached for his hand. "It's OK." I couldn't help but smile at him.

"You're holding hands." Pearl said dryly. "You *do* know that, right?"

We all laughed, but I pulled my hand away, my cheeks burning.

*

Later that night, Ben and I were back in the Control Room. We sat together facing the central main screen, with the smaller screens to either side of it still in darkness, when Ben pressed the button and suddenly the large screen was lit with a bright green light.

"That's what night vision does," Ben explained. "It lights the image so brightly that you can actually operate The Eye in the Sky as if it was daylight. See?" He used the controls to move the drone backwards and forwards, upwards and downwards. The image was very clear. I could see the outdoors barracks and identify each building very clearly.

"It's a bit trickier on people, though," he said. "Faces look a bit weird through night vision, but once you get used to it, you will be able to track and trace, just like in daytime. Shall we try?"

I nodded enthusiastically.

Ben made a gesture for me to take over the controls. I took over the drone and raised it up high into the night sky. Everything was brightly lit, trees, buildings, and a few vehicles. There were no people around. As the bunker was so isolated from anywhere else, finding someone to watch and trace at this time of night demanded that I drive it far into the horizon, in the hope of being able to find someone. For a few minutes all we saw was just barren earth, a few craters, random houses here and there, but no people. I was getting tired, maybe a little disappointed, and certainly impatient, and so the drone under my control was flying faster and faster, to the point that the image of the ground was becoming a bit of a blur.

"STOP! STOP! Go back!" Ben jumped out of his seat.

I saw it too. I swear I saw it too.

"Back, back!"

"I am driving it back… I can't see it!"

"Did you see it? Just before?"

"Yes!"

We were both frantic around the controls. Slowly we scanned the area inch by inch, but the thing was gone.

We sat back in stunned silence.

"What do you think that was?" I asked Ben, embarrassed that we missed seeing the thing clearly due to my rush.

"I don't know. I haven't seen anything like it before." He said, confused.

"It was… alive," I whispered.

"Yes."

"Like… a beast."

"You mean like the beasts of the past?"

"Wouldn't you say?"

"I suppose you're right. It did look a little bit like that. I'm not good with what beasts looked like to be honest."

"Haven't you seen images of them? In books?" I was surprised by that. I used to dwell over these old books as a child, wishing, hoping against hope, that one day the beasts would return.

"Maybe, as a kid. Not recently. Not with interest. They're all gone anyway…" Ben said gingerly.

The catastrophes that wiped out nearly everything off the face of this wretched planet, took with it almost anything living. Only a fraction of humanity survived, some insects, but the beautiful beasts that shared the planet with us, they were all gone.

"But maybe… not all?" I wondered out loud.

"How can it be possible?"

"I don't know."

"Have we recorded any of it, by chance?" Ben's question was hypothetical. We didn't. it was only a training session. Training sessions were not recorded.

We kept searching for the thing but found nothing. "Maybe we only imagined it," he said, finally. Maybe we did.

Eventually, we returned the drone to the bunker. Both heavy hearted.

"Sorry we couldn't see people," Ben said kindly. "It's difficult to find them from where we are sometimes."

I nodded. I was tired.

"But hey, maybe we can view older recordings, just so you can see what it looks like?"

I was eager to ask him to let it go. Maybe we should do it again tomorrow night. But somehow, spending a few more moments with Ben in the Control Room, even as tired and disappointed as I felt, was a more appealing option than going back to my room. So, I nodded with as much enthusiasm as I was able to display, careful not to yawn.

With several key presses and commands, Ben displayed the archived files on the screens, with what was quite an impressive, renewed energy. Maybe he didn't want to end the session either. That thought pleased me.

There were a few night clips that we could pick from. Ben skimmed through them very quickly, until finally we saw people on the screen.

"Yes!" Ben exclaimed, triumphantly.

The screen was alight with bright green. I could see the people very clearly. Two of them. They were running. Even from up high, overlooking them from above, I could see their faces. I could see… a man and a woman. I could see… I could see their faces! I could see! My mother!

"Mum and David!" I blurted in shock.

Ben's face sank in horror. He darted to the control board and paused the clip.

"I'm sorry, Sunny. I'm such an idiot, I should have thought about that before, I'm so sorry!"

"Press play, Ben." I whispered.

"Sunny, I…"

"Play it, Ben. Please."

He sighed and hesitated, but eventually he pressed the play button.

There they were, right under my fingertips. My mother. Beautiful Stella. Her copper-red hair dark green due to night vision, but her face still so strong. "Mum," I whispered. Tears started pooling in my eyes. Ben reached for my hand. I didn't pull it back. It gave me the strength I needed to keep watching. Mum and David were running, then suddenly they stopped and turned around. A couple of topless vehicles stopped not too far away from them. A man and a woman were marching towards Mum and David. They were holding guns… I know this woman. I'd know her anywhere, with green light, with red light, with no light. It's Jacqueline Roth. Roth and the other man were getting closer to Mum and David. Their guns drawn. I could see Mum and David were saying something to each other. I watched their lips. *I love you*. Then, the guns fired. I jumped in my seat; a scream escaped me. Tears were streaming freely down my face. "No! No! No!" Mum and David both fell to the ground. The image cut back into darkness.

"I'm so sorry, Sunny," Ben whispered. His eyes were filled with tears.

Suddenly I filled up with a burning rage. "This woman, this *murderer*, she's here! She's right here! Being cared for by *our* people. It's crazy! It isn't right!" I grabbed the controls and rewound the clip to the point when the guns fired. "See? She's a murderer! How can you *turn* a murderer? How can you make an evil person un-evil? She sent the body of my best friend to be 'processed', whatever that means. This woman is evil! And we are going to trust her?"

Ben nodded in silence. He bit his lips, then said quietly, "I'm so sorry, Sunny. I understand your anger." And then, he hugged me.

In my overflowing emotional turmoil, I sank into him, and from the depth of my soul, I started crying, my body heaving in uncontrolled misery, shock, pain, and anger. Ben's shirt was soaked with my tears and dribble, but even if I was aware of it, I couldn't control it, and I couldn't stop it. Still, he kept hugging me, until finally I could take in some air and regain control of myself. Only then he released me, staying very close as I wiped my tears and took deep, calming breaths in.

"I don't know how they are going to *turn* her," I said, Finally, "and maybe they can... I don't know... do this magic... but I'm telling you right now, Ben, that I will *never ever* trust this woman. Ever."

5.

For three months I avoided going anywhere near the Medical Ward. I didn't want to see Roth, not even by chance. From Nathan, who was always in the know, I learned how nicely she was recovering. That she had surprised all the medics and was now breathing without aid. Truly, a miracle child!

I sensed that my avid resentment to this whole Operation 'Let's Turn The Witch To Our Side' was starting to rub people the wrong way. Even my close friends were finding it hard to keep listening to my complaints and warnings. So, I started keeping my thoughts to myself. Her being there, in the bunker, her becoming part of us, it had already been decided. There was nothing I could have done about it.

I spent all my time honing my mission skills. My shooting precision greatly improved, and my one-on-one combat ability was becoming quite impressive. I could disarm an opponent in less than 30 seconds, even Bill. Somehow, all these challenges became a walk in the park once I imagined Jacqueline Roth in front of me. While my explosives-making skills were still lacking somewhat, my Eye in The Sky manoeuvring was becoming very smooth. I just kept looking for the thing I saw that night, with Ben. And every now and then I brought out the recording of my mother and David from the archives, and watched them being shot to death, again, and again.

It was around that time, one late morning, as I was making my way to the small gym, that I saw Jonathan walking towards me. Since coming to the bunker, I hadn't seen Jonathan, Rose or Spirit, my little family, and I missed them terribly. Initially, I couldn't quite believe it. What was he doing here? But as soon as I was sure it was him, I just ran straight into his arms.

"Jonathan!"

"Heeey Sunny," he said in his deep, soft voice, his hug wide and warm and generous.

"It's so good to see you again." My face was squashed into his big chest, my words slightly muffled.

"You too, lovey." There was a smile in his voice.

I squeezed him tight before I let go. "Are Rose and Spirit here too?"

"No. Just me."

"Oh." *Why didn't they come? Is Spirit still mad at me for leaving?*

I linked his arm in mine. "Let's go to the kitchen, we can drink some tea and have a chat." The kitchen in the bunker also served as a dining room.

He hesitated. "Actually, Sunny, there's something I must do first. How about I meet you there in a couple of hours?"

"Oh. Yeah, sure. Ok." Only then it dawned on me that I wasn't at all the reason he was there. It hurt me, but also confused me. Why was he there, then?

Jonathan kissed my head. "See you in the kitchen. Save me some biscuits." And he was gone.

Two hours still left me enough time to visit the gym, but my heart was no longer in it. I ran for twenty minutes, lifted a few weights, then promptly returned to my room to change before my meeting with Jonathan.

"That wasn't very long." Pearl wasn't impressed by my quick return from the gym. She was sitting in front of our small mirror, trying to get her beautiful, thick, black curly hair into a bun. "Is the rowing machine broken again? I told them to fix it. I told them, like a hundred times!"

"It's not the rowing machine." I said and giggled. To be honest, working out on that machine was Pearl's thing, not so much mine. "Jonathan is here. I'm meeting him in the kitchen soon."

Pearl was eyeing me through the mirror. "Just him, or the family?"

"Just him."

"Huh."

"He's here for another reason, not me."

"Huh." She gave up on her hair and turned to face me. "Must be Jacqueline Roth."

"What do you mean?"

"That must be the reason he's here."

"No way. What? No!"

"Well, he's a doctor ain't he?"

"But…"

"I'm telling ya. It's that."

No. No way. It couldn't be why. It made no sense at all. No sense.

"I'm here to help Alec with the treatment of Jacqueline Roth," Jonathan said almost immediately after we sat down at the table, our simple tea mugs steaming.

One-Nil to Pearl.

But why? Even him? I truly had zero allies on this issue.

"But, why?" my cheeks were burning hot, and I wasn't sure if because of my anger or because of the steaming tea.

"Medically, I can help. They asked me, so I came."

"But this is the woman who shot you! Don't you remember that? She could have killed you if not for the heavy-duty frame you put under your shirt!"

"I know. I remember."

"You wouldn't have known that she was going to shoot you if not for my weird dream!" The night before Jacqueline Roth came to abduct me from the beach house, I had one of those odd dreams where my mother visited me and warned me about things. She showed me how Jonathan was going to be shot. When I woke up, I immediately warned him. My dreams were like omens, but I haven't had those kinds of dreams in a very long time.

"I know. You saved my life." His voice was soft.

"Then why would you help the woman who tried to kill you and Rose? The woman who was chasing me and Spirit to take us back into slavery. Why?"

"I took an oath."

"What oath?"

"A medical doctor's oath. I must help, if I can."

I shook my head in disbelief. "How can a stupid oath be more important than us?"

"It isn't. Sunny, love, you are no longer in any danger."

"Everyone keeps saying that, but how can you be so sure?"

"Because it is so. It is the truth. You will see it for yourself, eventually."

In my frustration, I gulped my tea and burned my tongue.

"And how are you doing, Sunny? How are you managing your life here, as an activist?"

Suddenly I didn't feel like talking. I wished that Jonathan would go away.

"I'm fine." I said, sulking, my tongue stinging.

He smiled. His smile so kind and full of love. Was I being irrational? He would never do *anything* to hurt me. So maybe I should trust him, and Violet, and everyone else who are so sure this deal with Roth could work.

"You look fantastic. Radiant." He said.

I gave him half a smile. "How's Spirit? And Rose?"

"They are both wonderful. Spirit misses you, but she is doing really well. You know Spirit, she is such a happy, confident child. She is filling our house with her artwork," he said with a small laugh, "her artwork is beautiful. very accomplished. We're very proud of her."

I sensed my eyes tearing up.

"Rose sends you her love, of course. I'll need to give her a very detailed description of how you look and how you're doing, no doubt." He smiled.

I smiled back. I couldn't stay mad at him. My heart ached for being away from them.

"I miss you all." I said, rubbing my tears roughly with my hands.

"We miss you too, Sunny, very much." His eyes were so kind.

"Oh, before I forget, I have something for you!" he shuffled in his seat and dug a small parcel out of his backpack. It was wrapped in paper and tied with a slim stringy rope. "It's from Spirit."

My fingers trembled as I slowly opened the parcel. Inside the paper wrap lay a little necklace. No more than a small shell attached to a string.

"She made it for you," he said.

It was beautiful.

"Here, let me help you put it on." He quickly stood up and helped me tie the necklace around my neck, as I pushed my hair out of the way.

I never had any jewellery. Wearing something around my neck felt strangely unfamiliar, but knowing I had something of Spirit resting so close to my heart, made me happy. I traced the shell's curves with my finger. It felt nice.

"Please tell her that I absolutely love it, and I'll never take it off."

He nodded.

I walked him up to the surface, where his new car was waiting under a camouflaged parking space.

"You know, you can always come home, don't you, Sunny? If you ever change your mind about being here."

I nodded and smiled. "I know. I don't think I'll change my mind."

He smiled back. "No, I didn't think so. But you could come visit. I asked Violet to allow you to come. Initially there's a whole issue of keeping you here so you aren't conflicted between home and activism, but I don't think this is an issue for you. And Spirit would love to see you. So would Rose and I of course."

I was deeply happy to hear that. If any news could offset the surprise of Jonathan helping Roth to recover, this was it. "I'd love to come. I'll get something organised."

"Oh, and Sunny," Jonathan added just before he drove off, "I want you to know that we are all very proud of you!"

6.

A few more uneventful months passed in the bunker, until one day, at lunchtime, Nathan eagerly took his seat at what has become 'our' table, and before any of us had a chance to take a bite of our lunch he gushed, "So, I heard a new mission is up!"

"Yes!" Ben high-fived him, excitedly.

"How do you know?" Pearl was not going to get herself too excited about a rumour.

"I've heard."

"From whom?"

"Violet and Peter were talking."

"So, you were eavesdropping?"

"You can say that." He smiled brightly and winked at her.

"I'll believe it when it's formally announced," she said, unimpressed, and dived into her lunch.

"So, what is it going to be? Did you hear any details?" Ben was obviously thrilled.

"Ummm... these Cauliflower and Kumara patties are so goooood!" Pearl's attention was already elsewhere. Her eyes were closed as she savoured the flavours of her lunch. I was tempted to start eating as well. The patties really did look amazing. But I wanted to know more about the mission.

"Woollies," Nathan said as he took a big bite. "Oh, man, these *are* good!"

"What's woollies?" I asked, my eyes skipping between the three of them.

"They're grown for their hair," Ben explained. "Kept in terrible conditions, shaved frequently, it's pretty horrible."

"Their hair?" that sounded so implausible, I wondered if he was kidding.

"Imagine Pearl's hair, only fifty times thicker," Nathan said with a smile.

I've never seen anyone with thicker hair than Pearl's, so fifty times thicker was pretty hard to imagine.

"And they all look the same," Pearl decided to join in the conversation after all. "Sickly looking things."

"They're not things. They're beings, like us." Ben corrected her.

"That's what I said."

Ben rolled his eyes and smiled at me.

We hadn't even finished eating our meal before Peter, who was Violet's closest assistant, a strongly built man, rather short and heavily bearded, walked into the kitchen and in his booming voice announced, "Can I have your attention folks, please!" Gradually, perhaps even reluctantly, all vibrant conversations died down and silence ensued. "Thank you. Everyone, please present yourselves in the community room at four pm sharp for an announcement about our next mission and… a few other things. Don't be late please! Thank you."

"See, I told you!" Nathan smiled triumphantly.

"A few other things… what d'ya reckon that is?" Pearl asked and continued licking her spoon, her dessert bowl of vanilla almond ice cream nearly empty.

"A new cleaning shifts roster?" Nathan suggested.

I kept myself busy devouring my ice cream, nose down, spoon busy. I knew what it was. It had to be it. And by the way Ben was staring at me, he was thinking the same.

*

Ben and I were on kitchen cleaning shift after lunch. Most people hated it, but I found scrubbing pots and pans in the warm pool of water was actually quite relaxing.

"Why so serious?" he asked me, standing close, busy towel-drying the dishes I'd just washed. Standing *very* close. I loved the smell of him. I loved the shape of him. Oh dear. I needed to keep my mind off him. There was a mission ahead. I had to focus!

He picked up a cluster of soap bubbles from the top of the sink and blew them my way. It made me chuckle. "Stop it or I'll whip you with my towel…"

"That is not a threat, I hope?" He chuckled back, and gently whipped me with the hand towel he was drying the dishes with.

"Oh yeah? Is that all you've got?" I grabbed the towel I'd already tossed onto the laundry basket and whipped him around his waist.

A whipping war ensued, both of us giggling like two naughty children. Around and around the kitchen we danced with our towels slapping and lashing, nothing too rough, but with much intent. Then, suddenly, as my arm was raised for a thrash of my towel, he moved close and grabbed my arm, his face an inch from mine, both of us breathing hard, our gaze fixed deeply into each other's eyes. The moment was so intense, it sent bolts of electricity down my spine.

"Sunny, I…."

"Oh, sorry… didn't mean to interrupt." It was Miley, one of the best snipers in the bunker, although you wouldn't guess it from her very girlie appearance. She backtracked from the kitchen, smiling apologetically, "Only came to grab some water…"

With bashful smiles Ben and I stepped away from each other. In silence we quickly finished putting away the clean, dry dishes, and awkwardly parted ways until the afternoon announcement.

At three fifty-five in the afternoon the community room was crowded with eager activists. By the time Pearl and I walked in, all available seats were already taken, so we positioned ourselves on the floor. I quickly skimmed the room to see if Ben and Nathan were already there but couldn't trace them anywhere.

"Don't bother looking, Nathan is always late, *always*, and Ben is probably with him." Pearl said, checking her wristwatch.

At exactly four o'clock Violet marched into the room, followed by Peter. The wide doors closed behind them, only to be frantically opened again by Nathan, Ben in his footsteps, sneaking into the room and silently placing themselves against the back wall, as if no one had noticed them being late.

"See?" Pearl whispered, with a classic 'told you so' look.

Peter opened the meeting. "Thanks for being here everybody. I know you were all waiting impatiently for our missions to pick up again. It's been several months now, and some of you were wondering why we had nothing planned yet. We'll get to that soon, but I just want to firstly acknowledge your patience and your commitment, for doing your shifts and taking part in keeping our quarters presentable, and for keeping yourselves fit and ready. Now, we all know that a total liberation is not something that can be achieved in a day, or just due to a single campaign. It's a long marathon, not a sprint, and there are many challenges for us yet to face. But there are some wins, and all the signs point to the beginning of a seismic shift against the industries of exploitation. We had news from other cells up north and overseas, doing an excellent job putting real pressure on some of the biggest companies in the dairy and meat industries. The financial decline of these companies proves that we are winning, but as we get stronger, so might the pushback. We must expect and be mentally prepared for some backlash. A backlash could take many forms. Our few allies within the police force could turn against us, we could be raided and arrested, more obstacles could be put in our way, both by the industries of exploitation and by the public who supports them, and wrong perceptions could cause the generous supporters who finance our operations to pull out. These are but a few examples. There are many ways our fight for total liberation could be made more difficult." He paused and looked around. While his face was mostly beard, his ice-blue eyes fiercely glinted, and his look was stern. *This man must feel no fear at all,* I thought.

"In this fight for total liberation, we are strong, but still outnumbered. So, we must grab and use every opportunity we can get, to even the odds on the battlefield. And I mean *every opportunity.*" Peter's eyes rested on me, as he continued. "We must trust our judgement, and manipulate the game as far as we can, because otherwise, the road to total liberation might be much longer than it needs to be, and much more brutal."

People were nodding in agreement, even though most had no idea yet that he was actually referring to a very specific 'opportunity'. A very specific 'manipulation of the game'. But I did, and I knew that while addressing everyone in the room, he was talking to me.

"So, it is time we made it public knowledge that several months ago we took a high-ranking hostage." He paused to allow for some excited murmurs. "From no other but Natures!" An eruption of claps and cheers made him smile. Peter smiling was an odd scene. It looked like his beard had cleaved, presenting two rows of bright teeth. "She was shot by one of our own". Pearl sneaked me a triumphant look. "We brought her here, and since then she has been recovering slowly and nicely. Moreover, the real news here is, that with the gentle but firm expertise we have had for many years, we believe that we have managed to successfully turn her!" Now the room was a cacophony of loud cheers, roars, whistles, and excited conversations. "Calm down, calm down everyone." His tone was commanding, and soon enough the room's attention was his again. "She still isn't ready to be presented to you all quite yet, but very soon we'll have a gathering just for that. I need you to be open-minded about this…" again, he was looking directly at me, "and trust us with our judgement. This is good news people. Very good news." Clapping broke out here and there. "So now, after investing a lot of effort into this new prized possession, we can finally get back on track and plan new missions. Soon enough we will obtain a lot of inside information from this woman, and we'll be able to plan bigger and more daring actions. But this is still in the future. Our next mission is one we wanted to action last year, but we put it on hold for all sorts of operational reasons. We're ready now to kick-start it again. I'll let Violet talk about the mission and the next steps."

Violet, who thus far allowed Peter to take centre stage, stepped forward. She was lean, quite fit and toned, with an air of strength and self-confidence. Her face was ageless, though she must have been older than my mother. I wondered if she was Rose's older or younger sister. Both so different. Violet was by nature a leader. Rose a carer. I loved both these women, but with Violet, as close as I felt towards her, I realised that there was very little I knew about her. What brought her to where she was? What made her happy? Did she like to read? Did she enjoy music? Does she have someone special? Rumours persistently insisted that she and Alec, our surgeon and medic, had a *thing*. It might have been true, but there were no public giveaways to that effect, as far as I could notice. But maybe I just didn't know how to pick up on these signs. I had zero experience with such things.

"Good afternoon, everyone. Thank you, Peter, for updating us with the exciting news. Hopefully we will introduce you to our new 'recruit' within a few weeks." The way she said 'recruit' was deliberately sarcastic, which made people chuckle. "But now we move on to business. Our next mission is a rescue mission and disruption in a Woollies farm." Claps of excitement across the room. "Our aim is to destroy their breeding premises, and to liberate as many as we can. Detailed planning begins tomorrow morning at eight am in the Board Room. For that first planning session, the following people must attend: Bill, Miley, Leah, Bryan, Suli, Jessica, Ben, Nathan, and Pearl. Everyone else can come if they'd like, it's not obligatory for you if I haven't mentioned your name. Everyone will be participating in the mission, but if you're not one of the people I called by name, it simply means you're not a core decision maker for this one. Is everyone clear?" Nods all around. "Excellent. Off you go, then."

She didn't mention my name.

"Don't worry about it," Pearl was quick to comfort me. "It doesn't mean much. It takes a while before you get the chance to be a core team member, and even then, you're not called for absolutely everything."

I work so hard, and I'm still not good enough.

Before Pearl and I had the chance to get up from the floor, Ben and Nathan were right there with us, Ben's arm reaching for me, to help me up. I grabbed it and hopped to my feet.

"Why can't *you* give me *your* hand?" Pearl teased Nathan as she pulled herself up, all Ooohs and Ouchs.

"Because you might bite it off?" he teased her back.

"Hey, don't be upset for not being called," Ben confirmed what Pearl just told me. "It means nothing. Sometimes you're in the core team, sometimes you're not."

"You don't think it means I'm not ready?" I wondered out loud. I needed honesty.

"It could be that you just haven't been here long enough. But not necessarily. It's definitely not personal, you know, because of the 'new recruit'," he gestured with his hands to show that he was merely quoting Violet. We all smiled. "I think you should come anyway. You can still be there. See how it's done. You can learn a lot from a meeting like that."

"Yeah, you should come," Pearl agreed, and Nathan joined in by nodding.

"Ok, I might do that," I said, sounding unsure, but in my mind, I'd already made the decision to be there.

7.

At half past six the next morning Pearl woke me up. We exercised a little in our room, had breakfast, and at five minutes before eight we were already seated in the Board Room, with most of the others. Ben arrived a couple of minutes after, his face lit up when he saw me there. At eight o'clock Violet and Peter walked in.

"Good morning, everyone." Violet smiled and looked around. "I'm glad to see you here, Sunny," she said, "If our friend Nathan fails to arrive within the next five minutes, you'll become a core member in his stead."

But before I had a chance to rejoice, my chances were quashed by a puffing Nathan, bursting into the room. "Sorry, Boss," he said as we all sniggered.

Violet waited for him to grab a seat, and then, with a couple of button presses on the wall, a sky image appeared. "Hopswich-Chizzle & Sons. We'll call them Hops; I'm not going to break my teeth over this. A woollie farm we've been watching for a while. About sixty minutes' drive to the east. Their so-called welfare rating is shocking, to those who give a hoot about welfare, rather than liberation. A couple of years ago the valley was flooded, and we have reasons to believe that quite a lot of the woollies drowned. As you can see, it appears that only two of the five buildings show signs of fecal activity." She pointed at some dots around the buildings.

"Those are piles of shit," Pearl whispered in my ear.

"This thing here," Violet pointed with her purple marker, "is probably a mass grave. But it seems Hops are a bit lazy to be digging, because these," she pointed at another spot on the sky image, "are bodies."

I felt sick. In all my time being a dairy slave, and after everything I'd been through, I never realised there were places so much worse than Natures. To live an entire life of misery and abuse, only to die without dignity, your body tossed on the ground, not even buried.

"The good news is that the place isn't fenced. The bastards are so sure of themselves, they're not expecting woollies to escape. And I imagine that for every woollie they lose, they get compensated, if they can blame the weather for it."

"Why don't they escape?" I asked. All eyes were on me. Clearly, it wasn't acceptable to ask questions before the presentation was over. "Sorry, I didn't mean to interrupt."

Violet smiled. "Woollies are sun sensitive; they can't wonder off during the day or they will fry themselves to death. The valley isn't shaded. At night they are probably locked in."

A life without hope. Can there be anything worse?

"Apart from these two buildings, our key target is this ugly big building right here," Violet pointed to an ugly big building slightly further away from the elongated ones where the Woollies were kept. It painfully reminded me of The Shed. "This is their breeding premises. I imagine there are all sorts of hellish machines in there, a rape rack and all such glorified 'humane' torture gadgets. It's also where they keep their genetically modified embryos, so it's a bit of a

54

lab." She paused, drank some water, then continued. "This here is the shearing shed. I'm expecting it to be covered with blood and scalp matter. Don't be surprised if they sometimes just chop a whole head off instead of shearing it, as this little thing you see here," she zoomed the image closer and pointed at something white and small, "is a skull."

I gulped some water to stop myself from fainting. I had no idea. No idea. How low have we stooped as humans to be doing this to other, sentient beings?

"Any questions?"

"How many are we looking to liberate?" Bill always looked sophisticated with his white hair and beard.

"As many as we can. There is a sanctuary that will take them all, and if any of them prefer a life of an activist after what they've endured, they'll be welcome to join us."

"Any more questions?"

I raised my hand again. "Violet, you said that based on the, uhm *poo* piles," I still wasn't used to using words like 'shit' quite as comfortably as Pearl did, "those two buildings are the ones inhabited. But… don't you think that the woollies would have gone to, you know, do *that*, as far as possible from where they sleep? Which means, these two might not be where they are, but where they are not?"

Violet nodded. "Fantastic observation, Sunny. Great question. But if you look at how the piles are ordered, you'll see that each pile is positioned right in front of a tiny hole in the wall, which is a sorry excuse for a window. So, my guess is, that they defecate inside, either in a bucket or without, and toss it out the window." It was unfathomable. It is against any natural instinct to defecate where you sleep, yet they had no choice. And she said that they might not even have a bucket. How then? With their bare hands? The thought was gruesome beyond imagining.

"Which brings me to another point," Violet continued, "Those who liberate the Woollies from their quarters should expect the absolute worst conditions. The worst stench, the worst filth. There could be many sick and wounded, we will bring them here for treatment. Some could be too sick to move, we'll need a lot of people to help mobilise them."

"Where is the staff during the night?" This question came from Suli, an elegant woman who must have been about Violet's age, her pretty, short hair peppered with grey, accentuating her mocha brown skin and mesmerising hazel eyes.

"Great question. The truth is, we just don't know. There are no obvious staff buildings. Either staff go home for the night, or they are on the premises, but we don't know where. This is an important issue, because it means we need snipers all around."

"Music to my ears!" Miley rejoiced. Her shooting skills were without parallel.

"Yes, I thought you would enjoy that, Miley," Violet smiled.

"Do they speak our language?" Pearl jumped in with her own question.

"They should, but you must expect them to fear us. They may not communicate with us until much later. If you tell them we're there to liberate them, they should understand, but again, anything is possible."

Pearl took some notes in her notebook. *I should bring mine next time.*

"OK, I'm opening the floor to your ideas for mission outline."

Starting with Peter, one by one they walked to the wall to suggest their ideas for how to accomplish the mission. Each person suggested a way that suited their own strength. Snipers proposed a plan that was armed to the teeth with long distance precision guns, while combatants preferred a strong ground mission, and the explosive experts wanted to see the entire place ablaze. Only a couple of them proposed a well-balanced approach, one of them, to my delight, was Ben. There were disagreements, challenges, arguments, but it was all done in a collaborative and very amicable manner. I was so moved to sense the deep respect they all shared for one another.

Discussions dragged throughout the day. Lunch was brought in, to save us from going to the kitchen. By nightfall, a rough plan had been formulated. Teams were put together, each with a set of tasks and assigned personnel. The next day, training started in earnest. I was assigned to team Alpha One. Our key target was liberating Woollies from building one. Ben was assigned as Alpha One's lead. We started training at nightfall, on the surface. The old, deserted military barracks served as our prop and backdrop. Everything was very formal. There was no room for error. Lives were at risk. Many lives. We tried simulating various scenarios where something went wrong, knowing all too well, we couldn't prepare for absolutely anything. We made a lot of mistakes. In one training session we liberated the wrong house, in another, we were ambushed, in another lost our comms. One thing we found out very quickly, is that we couldn't trust the availability of enough natural light, not even with a full moon. Cloudy skies meant compromised vision. We had to use night vision goggles. Getting used to seeing everything in bright shades of green took getting used to, and often it happened that we stepped over one another, or ran into each other.

Learning from those mistakes made us better prepared, but also more nervous. We weren't superhumans. We were just ordinary people, trying to do the right thing.

8.

Two weeks after we started preparing for the mission, an announcement was made that at 4:00 pm in the afternoon, everyone should present themselves at the Community Room. The 'new recruit' was about to be revealed. By coincidence, it was also the day I'd celebrated exactly eight months since joining DaSLiF. All my efforts to become suddenly morbidly sick failed. I was fit as a fiddle and had absolutely no excuse not to attend. Except maybe, that this was the woman who killed my mother, a minor fact everyone seemed to be forgetting.

In spite of my best efforts, my feet became so heavy, I needed all my will power to make it to the community room on time. But I was late. Later even than Nathan. I saw him sneaking into the room while I was still far back in the corridor telling my feet to march on.

As soon as I opened the door, I saw her, sitting slightly sunken in a wheelchair, her feet covered with a blanket. She was even thinner than before, all skin and bones, and very pale. Her hair that used to be so tidy, short, with the fringe always neatly combed to one side, was now shapeless, messy. Truly, she was a sorry sight, and still her presence, the very air of her, made me nauseous. As I made my way across the room our eyes instantly locked. A multitude of emotions darted inside me. *She's here to kill me. She's here to finish the job.* Her eyes followed me all the way until I sat down on the floor next to Pearl. Roth was smiling. *What was she smiling about? I'll tell you what, the prey just fell straight into her lap that's what.*

"She doesn't look all high and mighty anymore, eh?" Pearl whispered to me.

No, maybe she didn't, but her current sorry state meant nothing. The woman was evil.

"Welcome everyone," Violet said to the room, looking straight at me. "I'm glad you all could make it." My entire body was itching to get out of there. Where was Ben? I quickly scanned the room. He was sitting on the sofa to my left. His eyes were on me.

"Without further ado, I'm happy to introduce you to Jacqueline Roth."

Murmurs of awe and surprise filled the room. She was well known in activists' circles. Her ruthless reputation preceded her.

"We captured Jacqueline eight months ago, during a mission to protect one of our own. She was shot and very badly wounded. It was touch-and-go whether she'd survive or not. Indeed, it's a great opportunity to thank Alec for working so hard and making the impossible possible, by saving her life." People clapped, even though Alec wasn't even there with us. It surprised me, almost to a point of giggling, to see Jacqueline Roth clapping too. *Rather out of character for the cold witch, I give her that.* "In the past eight months Jacqueline has made a remarkable recovery, and we are certain that very soon she'll be strong enough to walk again. We just need to fatten her up a little first, eh Jacqueline?" It was a lame jest, but Jacqueline Roth smiled widely at Violet and nodded. *What was going on with this show? Did the Roth woman lose her mind?*

"Also, during these last few months, Peter and I have worked very closely with Jacqueline, *showing* her, *encouraging* her and *helping* her to see that the values of life and freedom are the same for every living thing. We *assisted* her in seeing the world of forced exploitation and cruelty, that she was once a part of, for what it is: a vile relic of the past whose time was up."

Cheers and some yells of encouragement were kind of expected from the activists, but Roth, she was still smiling, and she was... clapping? *Was I awake?* I pinched myself to test that theory. *Yes, definitely awake.*

"I recognise this is not an easy transformation to make, and I know not everyone might be convinced," again, she was looking at me, "but I assure you that Jacqueline was tested again and again and has passed all our challenges with flying colours. She also agreed to work with us and help us with inside information that we could've only dreamed about getting otherwise. Her contribution to our missions will be invaluable, and we should all be thanking her and welcoming her to our organisation."

Violet turned to Jacqueline and shook her hand. Roth was still smiling. I doubt she had smiled that much over her entire life until eight months ago. People clapped and woo-hooed, excitedly conversing with each other. Tea and biscuits were brought into the room to allow us some sense of celebration.

I got to my feet, every bone in my body aching to wake from this farcical show. My head was spinning slightly. Suddenly, without having a chance to overthink it, somehow my feet were very decidedly making their way towards the woman in the wheelchair. I wasn't sure what I was doing, but the impulse to confront Jacqueline

Roth was just too strong.

I reached her in less than four large steps. Directly in front of her, I stood upright, armed with my best act of fake confidence, and looked her straight in the eyes. I said nothing, just stood and stared at her, waiting for cracks in her false display of new identity.

"Hello," she said to me, smiling widely, stretching her arm out to shake my hand. "What's your name?"

Seriously?

I didn't take her hand.

"I'm Sunny." I said with more than a tad hostility.

"Sunny. That's a very pretty name. A pretty name for a pretty girl." Still smiling at me, her hand slowly dropped to her lap, almost absentmindedly, as if she wasn't in the slightest offended by my refusal to shake it.

"I'm Stella's daughter." I said coldly. Playing my mother's name was the best card I had.

"Well, I hope your mother is very proud of you. She should be."

Was she drugged? This was enraging.

In some desperation, I leaned closer to her, and with a deep, lowered voice, whispered "I am One. One. Five. Seven. Two." This was the number that Roth herself gave me. Throughout the time she was chasing me, trying to capture and re-enslave me, she had never used my name. To her, I was nothing but a number. My eyes pierced her eyes, but there was nothing. Not a twinkle or registration, not a faint shadow of recognition, nothing. In fact, she started to look a bit scared of me.

"Sunny!" Violet interrupted. "What are you doing?"

"I'm introducing myself to J… to J… to Roth."

Violet took my arm and gently but decisively pulled me away.

"It was nice to meet you." Roth was calling after me.

"What were you doing?" Violet demanded.

"Like I said, I was introducing myself." I went for innocent, but it sounded more like bitter.

"She doesn't remember you."

"I don't believe it."

"Well, you should, because that's the truth."

"She's lying to you! She's playing you! Can't you see that?"

"No, I can't, and neither do the others. Sunny, accept it for what it is, this is not the Jacqueline Roth you remember!"

"If she suddenly has amnesia and can't remember me, how come she's supposed to give us inside information?"

"Because that is in her long-term memory. She remembers nothing of the past eighteen months."

I shook my head. I wasn't having a bar of it.

Violet sighed. She looked at me, then suddenly gave me a big hug. I wasn't expecting that, but unlike previous hugs, this one made me feel uncomfortable. I was still angry, and I needed straight answers, not hugs.

"Go, join your friends." She released me, and I left without a further word.

In my room, Pearl, Nathan, and Ben were already converged, waiting for my return. All I wanted was to throw myself on my bed and cry, but Ben was sitting there. As soon as I walked in, they were all at me, assaulting me with questions all at once. They were excited and curious, but to me right then, it sounded like a continuous, endless sentence, without any coherent meaning or reason. "WHATDIDYOUSAYTOJACQUELINROTHWHATDIDSHESA YTOYOUHATDIVIOLETWANTFROMYOU?

I ignored them all and dropped on the bed, back against the wall, cradling my feet in my arms, my head on my knees. I closed my eyes. I needed to disappear into myself for a while.

Immediately they all stopped talking. The silence in the room became thick and sticky and uncomfortable.

I sensed there was movement in the room, followed by the opening and closing of the door. *Good, I'm finally alone.*

"Would you like me to leave as well?" Ben's soft voice surprised me. SO, I wasn't all alone, after all.

"No. You can stay if you want." I whispered, my head still on my knees.

He scooted over and leaned on the wall next to me, his hand gently stroking my hair. It felt nice. I'm not sure how long he sat there like that, in complete silence, just softly stroking my hair. Maybe an hour. Maybe eternity. I was impressed at how well he could read me. I needed him to not talk to me. Just be there. And he was.

9.

From then on, Avoiding Jacqueline Roth became impossible. It seemed like everywhere I went, there she was, with her smiles. *What's with all the smiling?* At least during the nights, when we were preparing for our upcoming mission, I had some respite from her. Two weeks after formally joining us, Roth started walking. First with a cane, then independently. She was first in the kitchen at mealtimes, plainly enjoying the cruelty-free food she probably wouldn't have touched with a ten-foot pole in her previous life. Already she was looking stronger and healthier. But what really did my head in, was how people seemed to like her. There was never a shortage of people sitting with her at meals and chit-chatting, helping her get to her feet, giggling at some funny things she was saying. When had she become funny? Was a sense of humour also in her long-time memory?

I successfully maintained a fair distance from her and refrained from making any contact. At mealtimes I tried to always sit with my back to her, so I didn't have to see her. But I could always feel her long shadow on my back.

The mission was getting closer, and tension levels were rising. I was told it was natural before missions, to see people who were normally sociable and extroverted, suddenly seek the company of books and solitude. Generally, the atmosphere in the bunker turned more solemn and focused. In one such quiet afternoon, I was reading an old book that I borrowed from the library, Animal Farm by George Orwell. I found the book intriguing, because its protagonists were olden days beasts, but they were essentially acting more like people. Something about this book was oddly fascinating. I was sitting on the tattered sofa in the community room, my feet tucked under me, the book in my hands, safely shielded in my own bubble, when, in the corner of my eye, I observed the unimaginable eventuality of Jacqueline Roth taking a seat next to me. For a moment I thought I might be hallucinating, but no. She was there. *Go away, go away, go away!*

"Hi Sunny."

I put the book down, making every possible effort to show her I was annoyed.

"I'm sorry I'm disturbing you," she said with a smile. "Is this a good book?"

What do you want? "I like it."

She nodded. "Oh, good… good."

I looked at her, confused, irritated, and was contemplating to just get up and leave, when she suddenly said, "I wanted to apologise to you, Sunny."

"What do you mean?" *Murderer.*

"Violet told me what I did to you…. Before. She told me what I did to your mother. And to you, and your friends. I… I… I'm horrified at myself. I don't know what kind of person I was, I was… despicable." Her hands kept creasing and crumpling a piece of white tissue she was holding. "I… I can't even imagine… what you must think of me…" To my horror, Jaqueline Roth started to whimper. My jaw dropped. "I know you might never forgive me… and that's ok, Sunny, I honestly think, if I were you, I would probably not forgive someone like me... But I just want you to know, that if I could've gone back and change everything, I would... I just wanted to tell you I'm so sorry. I'm so sorry for what I've done... I can never make it up to you, but... I'm... I'm... I'm sorry..."

I was so shocked, I couldn't speak. Maybe *I* was the one going insane.

"Thank you for allowing me to talk to you. I won't disturb you further." She said nervously, padding her eyes with her tissue, and left.

I remained stunned and confused, and deeply irate. If this was an act, it was a very good one. Very polished. *Was it an act?* Surely, it had to be. How could someone who was so evil, so drained of any compassion, change so profoundly? I found it implausible that Jacqueline Roth, the Witch Queen of Natures, had suddenly turned to this goodie, smiley, soft, cuddly Aunty Roth. And what exactly did she think would happen now? That I'd just forgive her? That I'd just start trusting her? She'd say she was sorry, and we'd be best friends? I simmered on the sofa for a long hour thinking about this bizarre conversation over and over. A focused pain was starting to drill behind my eyes. Perhaps I *could* be slightly more civil towards her from now on, especially as my continuous resentment of Roth was making *me* the villain in the eyes of my peers, which was ridiculous. I realised that I had to play the game. But deep down, this conversation changed nothing, in fact, it only prompted me to be more vigilant.

One Year Since Joining DaSLiF

10.

The night air was crisp and slightly chilly and smelled of dry earth and crushed leaves. But inside, the bus smelled potently of leaked diesel and old rust. The hum of the engine was the only sound, as excitement and nerves chained our tongues. Darkness engulfed us, only the bus's yellow lights cut through, two elongated pools of light, surrounded by endless blackness. Nathan was driving. His black activist gear was concealed under a 'civilian' long-sleeved buttoned-up flannel shirt. A baseball cap on his head. Maybe that's how bus drivers were supposed to look? I couldn't tell. Our bus was one of three dispatched to the Woollie farm that night. Each bus left separately, each in a different route. Bill was driving the second bus and Jessica the third. I watched her as she hopped onto 'her' bus, taking the driver's seat, so easily manoeuvring the huge wheel. She waved at me as her bus left the barracks, like there was nothing to it. Underneath our seats our night vision gear and weapons rattled, reminding us of the potential danger we were about to put ourselves in. *What might happen to me if I get caught?* I pondered. *Would I be killed? Or would I be returned to Natures? I'd rather be killed than go back there.*

On and on the road stretched, partly smooth, partly rough and bumpy. My mouth was dry, my hands sweaty. *My first mission.* I couldn't stop thinking about the joy of liberating miserable souls from the pits of Hell. Slaves, like I used to be. Poetic justice. *I wish it was all done and dusted already.*

Before long, Nathan took a deep left turn, kept driving a while off road, then stopped the bus and switched the engine off. "OK folks, it's time to put your gear on, test our comms, get ready."

With bolts of excitement, we jumped to our feet, buckling gun belts, fastening night vision goggles, and pushing comms equipment into our ears.

"Alpha One to Omega, do you copy?" I could hear Ben's voice coming at once, both from the person next to me, and from the inside of my head thanks to the comms equipment in my ear.

"Omega to Alpha One, receiving you loud and clear, over." Peter's voice, carried into our heads from the Command Room far away in the bunker, was so clear, it was as if he was right there with us.

"Alpha Two to Omega, do you copy?" Bill was in my head now. The second unit parked in a different pitstop, to minimise any chances of our entire team being discovered or targeted.

"Omega to Alpha Two, receiving you loud and clear, over."

Silence.

We were expecting to hear Jessica next, but there was no sound. Long minutes stretched, and still no word from Alpha Three, our explosives unit for the mission.

"Omega to Alpha three, do you copy?"

Silence.

"Omega to Alpha Three, do you copy?"

Silence.

We shifted uncomfortably in our places. Dread was creeping into our hearts. What was keeping them?

"Eye One, what can you see?" Peter was talking to Leah, who was our Eye in the Sky. Both of them in the Command Room yet conversing through our heads.

Silence.

"Got them." Leah could be heard.

We couldn't tell what they saw in the control room, but clearly the drones located Jessica's bus.

"Alpha Three to Omega, do you copy?" Jessica's voice finally came through.

A sigh of relief vibrated through the bus.

"Omega to Alpha Three, receiving you loud and clear, welcome back, over."

We could hear Jessica giggle. "Wrong turn, sorry Omega." She was a mean driver, but not great with directions, apparently.

All units were in position. Each unit with its own tasks, and the snipers individually spread around us. Each team operated as an individual siloed mission, but only if we all did our jobs successfully, would the overall mission succeed. One by one we disembarked the bus. Adrenaline was rocketing through our bodies, and the urge to just get going was immense. But first, we formed a wide circle and embraced. It was a little ritual of co-empowerment and companionship, reminding us that we were all in it together. Ben was to one side of me, Pearl to the other. I could hear their rapid breathing, as they could hear mine. For a whole minute we stood embraced. It had a profoundly powerful calming yet motivating effect. As soon as the circle broke after a minute, the show was well and truly on the road. There was no going back.

11.

Running in total darkness, the world awash with false green light, my green friends running with me, I could tell we were getting closer by smelling the place even before seeing it. In missions to come, I learned that every place of horror had its own particular stench, a unique mixture of the sort of abominations specific to that place. But at the same time, they all had a common underlying stench they shared. The stench of death. You learn to recognise it immediately.

We all had personal protection facial masks, heavily soaked with breathable disinfectant, and sturdy gloves. The closer we got, so did the stench increase, tenfold. I pressed the mint-scented mask tighter to my nose. *How could people work here without fainting?* It was near impossible to comprehend. Maybe they got used to it. Building One was in plain sight now. It wasn't a large building at all, one story, elongated rectangle, with three tiny, filthy, barred windows along its long side. The building was made of plain wood, and what seemed from afar like old, peeling paint, on closer inspection turned out to be smears and smudges of who knows what. A heavy stench of rot and open sewage filled the air. Our movement stirred the many flies from their slumber, and they were now buzzing angrily around us, attempting repeatedly to get in my mouth, being bumped off by the mask, thank Mercy.

It suddenly struck me that the place was unusually silent. There were about thirty woollies kept in these facilities, and yet the complete silence was loud in its totality. The place was eerie and foreboding in a way that no amount of planning could have prepared us for.

We needed to circle the building to get to the door. Forming a line and crouching forward we moved around the building, careful not to step on faeces, or worse, bodies or skulls. Still, the ground felt revoltingly gooey and sticky. For a place that hadn't seen rain in weeks, this could not have been caused by rain. I dared not think what it *could* be.

We were just coming around the corner, energised by the prospect of reaching our target, when we saw him. The man.

He was seated on a simple chair right outside the shut and bolted door, his back leaning against the filthy wall. A singlet under an open flannel shirt revealed a large hairy belly. A wide-rim hat was covering his eyes. He was sleeping. *How on earth can anyone sleep in a place like this?* A large gun was resting by his side. Clearly, this man's job was to guard this place, or maybe to shoot any woollie who tried to escape. Possibly both.

There was no room for hesitation. We had to act quickly. Rushing forward, we needed to disarm him before he had any chance to shout out for help or get away. He didn't seem like much of a threat, sleeping on the chair with his big hairy belly, but looks can be deceiving. Before we could get any closer, the man jumped hastily to his feet, the gun in his arms, aimed straight at us. The guy was huge. Not just his belly, but in entirety. He was a giant. I'd never seen a person so tall and so wide in all directions.

"Who the fuck goes there?" He roared. His voice carried far into the valley's stillness.

He couldn't see us.

"Everything all right there, Tony?" It was another man, calling from further north-east. That must have been the guard of the second building. Alpha Two would have to deal with that other guy.

Our guy, Tony, took a few steps toward us. Soon enough and he would be able to see us. He loaded his gun and put it to his shoulder. *If he shoots, one of us could die.* Action was swift. In one move, Ben leaped forward and planted his foot in Tony's chest so hard, you could hear the ribs cracking. Tony tried to catch his balance but fell to his knees. Ben grabbed Tony's gun barrel and pointed it upwards, just as a solo bullet was fired. I rushed to Ben's aid and jumped behind Tony's massive neck, forcing both my arms around it. If he was devoid of air he'd faint. But the man was a machine. He shook his upper body so hard to get me off him, I was tossed like a rug doll, skidding away on the ground, deeply grazing my arm on what I hoped was gravel and not cracked skulls. I ignored the biting pain and jumped back to my feet, but in this split moment, Romesh, our strongest guy, was already behind Tony in my stead, sending a hard punch between his shoulder blades, then choking him to the point of unconsciousness. All the while Ben was standing with his gun aimed directly on Tony, in case even Romesh was no match for the giant. After a few long seconds of struggle, Tony snorted and fell limp to his side. There was no telling how long he'd stay out of action. Romesh grabbed Tony's gun, emptied it of bullets and tossed it far away.

We couldn't tell if Tony's single gunshot might result in more Tonies coming over with their massive build and firearms. We didn't know what was happening at Building Two, or the Breeding Lab. We had to proceed with our tasks regardless.

With a few silent hand gestures, Ben signalled to Romesh and Pearl that he wanted them to stay outside and keep guard, their guns facing outwards. Meanwhile I ran to the bolted door and smashed the lock with a couple of heavy smacks with the heel of my gun. Ben released the bolt, and I pushed the door open.

The smell that emanated from the room hit us like a physical force, making us both take a step back. It felt as if a hand had reached into my windpipe and squeezed it shut. Ben crouched to the side, removed his disinfectant mask, and gagged. His body heaved a couple of times with the spasms of disgust. He quickly got himself back up and faced the open door with me. Eyes. Terrified eyes. Terrified eyes and big hair. That's the first I could see. They were huddled together in one corner of the room, trembling in fear, physically shaking, but in total silence. We had to get in there, we had to get them out. I walked in. The woollies cowered further in the corner; some turned their faces away. They all looked so similar. Like a single person copied over and over to form different individual beings. And they were all female. That much was clear from the near see-through, filthy tunics they were wearing, and some weren't wearing even that little. I looked around. The room had nothing in it, only a single long shelf to sleep on, that wasn't long enough for all of them. No blankets, no pillows, no water, no buckets, nothing. But there were bodies. Three of them, one lying on the floor, the other two leaning against the wall. Their faces were so eaten up with rot, their noses and lips had completely vanished, and bits of skull could be seen through where once there was flesh. So worthless were they dead, that no one bothered to get these bodies out, to bury them. I gagged and pressed the mask tighter to my nose. The sooner we got out of there, the better. I reached closer to the woollies, but the closer I came towards them, the more they cowered. Not one of them was looking at me, not one dared to make eye contact. In a split-second decision, I took off my night vision goggles, and turned my flashlight on instead. With more hesitancy, I also removed the mask from my face.

"We're here to liberate you. To free you. Come with us!" the words fell heavily from my mouth, as I was speaking while at the same time struggling not to let the stench overtake me.

"Please, we must go, now! Come, you're going to be safe." it was Ben. His goggles and mask off, flashlight on, and like me, struggling to speak while holding his breath.

A few woollies looked at us now, but their eyes were blank, nearly lifeless. *Did they understand us? Did they understand what freedom was?*

"We're taking you away from here. No more pain!" I tried again.

Two of the woollies started showing signs of engagement. They separated from the huddle and looked at us. They were both very tall and painfully slim. When one of them spoke, we could hardly hear her, so weak and fearful she sounded. "Away from here?"

"Yes. Away from here."

"Help us?" she asked in amazement.

"Yes, we're here to help you." I reached my gloved hand out.

Instinctively, they both stirred away. With a heavy heart I realised that to these women, a hand reached out was never a good sign.

"Please…" I begged them, my hand still reaching out, because I didn't know what else to do. "Come. It's going to be OK."

Reluctantly, one of the two woollies took my hand. I smiled and slowly led her out. Seeing that their bravest friend was willingly coming with us, slowly those who could walk, followed. In silence, Ben and I led them out of the compound and into the bus. It was a painfully slow procession, as even those who could walk struggled on their feet. Our sniper's red eye followed us, ensuring we made it safely to the rusty bus. Nathan stood guard, as Ben and I went back to help carry those who couldn't walk. I was the last one to leave, the last remaining woollie leaning on me. I struggled to carry her. She was incredibly weak, but much taller than me, and part of her head was so deeply sliced, her wound was humming with maggots. I could practically *hear* them eating her up alive. Pearl and Romesh closed the procession from behind, their guns drawn. "Romesh. Help." I couldn't carry her any further. Romesh slipped himself underneath the woollie's arm and lifted her like she was paper. I swapped him for the back-guard position, my gun drawn, aimed into the vast darkness. I could feel my feet almost buckling underneath me from the effort to carry the wounded. With Romesh carrying the woollie so much faster, we were back at the bus in a few minutes. I was still panting. Romesh helped the woollie to a seat at the back, then hopped out again to swap positions with me once more. "Go, take a seat. Your arm is wounded." He said kindly.

Until he said it, I had completely forgot that I cut it when fighting

Tony. Now that my attention was back on it, the pain kicked in. I climbed up the narrow stairs and took a seat at the front.

"Alpha One to Omega, do you copy?"

"Omega to Alpha One, receiving you loud and clear, over."

"Omega, all matches are in the box, over," Ben said, using all the agreed, yet weird code names that *everyone* already knew, including those who might have intercepted our communication. So, in fact, using them was meaningless, but I suppose it sounded professional.

"Reading you, Alpha One, good job, over."

Before leaving the scene, we had to make sure all our people were safe. Nathan could drive the woollies back to base, but if other activists needed our assistance, the rest of us had to stay put and help them. The snipers drove enough individual vehicles to drive us all, should we need to separate from the bus.

All we were waiting for now, was to hear from Alpha Two and Alpha Three.

I looked back at the woollies, filling up the seats. All with the odd-looking blobs of thicker-than-thick, round hairdo. It was impossible to tell them apart. Their stunned, obedient silence nearly moved me to tears. They were on the cusp of a new life, such as they could never imagine.

"We're just waiting for the others." I whispered to them softly. One of them, possibly the brave one, nodded the smallest, faintest nod. They carried the room odour with them into the bus. As soon as we got back to base, they would know the luxury of a warm bath, maybe for the first time in their entire lives.

"Alpha Two to Omega, do you copy?" Bill's voice sounded rushed. He was panting.

"Omega to Alpha Two, receiving you loud and clear, over."

"Omega, all matches are in the box, over."

"Reading you, Alpha Two, excellent, over."

Phew! The relief was immense. Two teams out of three were ready.

One last team to go. Alpha Three were in charge of blowing up the breeding facility. Their time was spent wiring the place up to the rafters. Their blow-up cue was Alpha One and Alpha Two's confirmation that all woollies were removed from danger.

Within ten seconds the earth shuddered. The force of the explosion cut through the air, made the bus rock, the windows tremble, and our ears ring. A cloud of red fire rose to the sky from where the breeding facility once stood. The woollies could stay silent no longer. The blow up was so out of context and scary for them, they screamed, they groaned, kicked their feet and fell on the floor, yelling.

"It's ok. It's ok." I called to the brave one. "Look!" I pointed at the back window. "Look behind you. We blew it up."

Hesitantly, her hands still cupping her ears, she stood up and looked through the back window. Her eyes were ghost-like pale, but there was a soul in them. She understood me.

"Yah! Yah! Yah!" she called to her friends. It was a weird call, on the verge of a shriek. It was *their* call, and they all understood it. "Yah! They help us. They help. Observe." She pointed to the back window. Slowly all heads turned, their ghost-pale eyes taking in the scene of the place where they once knew so much pain, being consumed by fire.

"Alpha Three to Omega, do you copy?"

"Omega to Alpha Three, receiving you loud and clear, over."

"Omega, fireworks popped, over." Jessica sounded like she was enjoying every moment of it.

"Reading you, Alpha Three, well done, over."

That was it. We could go. A huge sense of relief washed over me.

With some festivity, Nathan switched the engine on. This was Romesh and Pearl's cue to get back in the bus.

But they weren't coming.

One banana. Two banana. *Where were they?* Three banana. Four banana. *What was the holdup?* From the back of the bus, loud gunfire broke the silence. Ben jumped up in alarm, "It's our guns." "Everybody, get down!" Nathan yelled to the woollies, as Ben and I rushed out of the bus, night vision switched on, guns drawn.

Bullets were flying in our direction from at least one location, a makeshift hide-out behind a few old barrels and a pile of junk. Romesh and Pearl returned fire, but they were exposed, and so were me and Ben.

"Alpha One to Red One, do you copy?" Ben's voice was full of alarm.

"Red One to Alpha One, loud and clear, copy." Miley responded.

"Red One we need red cover ASAP, over."

"Alpha One, reading you, over. Repositioning, over."

Miley's sniper position was not directed at the hideout, therefore she had to reposition herself to be able to help us. While she was getting into position, we were all sitting targets. Miley was quick, but not quick enough. A gun shot was fired from the hideout, and in a split-second Romesh dropped to the ground, doubled over with pain, grabbing his leg in his hands. "Son of a bitch!" he groaned. As I crouched by his side, 'ping' a bullet pierced the rustic metal of the bus, exactly where I was standing a second before. Someone in the bus screamed.

"Alpha One to Omega, we have a broken match, over." Ben tried keeping it together, but his voice gave away the urgency of our situation.

"Omega to Alpha One, reading you, over. Do you need more matches, over?" Somehow, Peter still sounded calm and in control.

"Omega, Keep matches at standby, over."

"Copy. Alpha Three, You're on standby, over."

"Alpha Three to Omega, roger that, over."

I checked out Romesh's leg. He was hit through his calf muscle. It didn't look good at all, and he was bleeding profusely. Without giving it a second thought, I took off my shirt and tied it around Romesh's lower knee, stemming the blood. Ben and Pearl kept shooting but couldn't penetrate the shooter's hide out. 'Plumpfffffff' a bullet hit the back wheel, just left of my shoulder.

C'mon Miley, C'mon!

A faint hiss in the air is all that we heard of the bullets that were fired from Miley's sniper gun. But the crush of heavy bodies and their screaming was hard to miss.

"Alpha One from Red One, your two hot ones are down, over."

The skirmish was over. Now we had to get out of there, but our wheel was shot.

Ben and I helped Romesh to the bus. Nathan was crouched next to the woollie who was shot. Seemed like it got her in her buttocks.

"The back wheel is fucked." Ben told Nathan with a desperate air. "Can we fix it?"

"We have a spare tyre. I can fix it, but I need everyone off the bus."

Ben nodded, defeatedly. He was sweating profusely.

"Alpha One to Red One, I need your red eye on the box, over."

"Red One to Alpha One, already on it, over."

Ben took his goggles off and wiped his forehead. "OK, here's what we're going to do, the wounded and those who can't walk stay on the bus. Sunny, I need you to lead everyone out and defend your location. Pearl, grab a couple of the Sleeping Gift syringes from the first aid kit and inject Romesh and the Woollie that was shot, then inject them with the coagulating solution so they don't bleed to death. When you're done, come out of the bus. Copy?"

"Copy" we said.

The prospect of the woollies climbing down and away from the vehicle that was going to take them to freedom and finding themselves back on the grounds of the place they were promised to leave, was hard to bear.

"It's going to be OK," I told the brave one and her carbon-copy friend. It's just a wheel." But I was nervous. The bus was falling apart as it was, and each wheel was massive. How long would it take?

Slowly, I led the woollies out of the bus, my gun drawn, my arm burning. They followed me, hesitant, defeated. Reluctantly, they sat themselves down on the ground, huddled together, as I circled them, my gun aiming into the dark. From the hide out two men were groaning. They were loudly shouting all sort of profanities at us. I don't know where Miley got them with her precise shots, but it clearly wasn't the mouth.

Pearl came out of the bus and joined the efforts to remove the old tyre and replace it with the spare. The minutes passed. The old tyre was finally off, now the new one had to be attached instead.

It's taking forever!

I could hear them all huffing and puffing, clicking, and banging, turning, and aligning.

Finally, the tyre was fixed. We could go.

Thank Mercy.

I watched the woollies as they slowly climbed back on the bus, holding to the hope that this time they'd be out of there. Silently and obediently, they sat down, waiting. It seemed like hours had passed, each minute dragging endlessly, but finally, Nathan switched the engine back on and we were on our way.

"Alpha One to Omega, sending matchbox back to base, over."

Back on the road, darkness came as a bliss. The open windows brought in some fresh cool air, and a sense of calmness. Suddenly I could feel the tension in my sore muscles, my wounded arm throbbing, my eyes heavy.

"Do you want some Sleeping Gift?" Pearl asked me, indicating my arm. "We have more."

"No, thanks. I'm fine. Save it for them." I pointed my head at the back of the bus, where Romesh and the wounded Woollies were all sleeping out their pain.

"You did really well tonight, Sunny." Ben said to me. "Absolutely brilliant."

I smiled at him. It was an exhausted smile, but also one full of relief and a sense of real accomplishment.

He then lowered his head closer to my ear, and whispered, "I also like your new style!"

It confused me for a second, but then I chuckled, as I remembered that from my waist up, all I was wearing was my black sports bra and Spirit's necklace. I leaned my head against his warm chest, and as if by magic, I fell asleep.

12.

As the bus entered the military compound it was lowered down to the underground parking via the camouflaged entrance. Bright LED lights flooded the bus. I was still hazy and disoriented, entangled in misty webs of sleep. I couldn't remember when I last slept as soundly as I did on the ride home, on Ben's chest.

"Rise and shine," he smiled at me.

"Your chest has a magical effect on me," I smiled in return, yawned, and stretched. My arm throbbed, shooing arrows of sharp pain all the way to my neck.

He smiled, his blue eyes twinkling.

I looked back at the woollies in the bus. They didn't appear to have moved an inch during the ride. The bright lights unsettled them.

"It's OK," I said to the brave one. "We're in a good place. The people here will help you."

She nodded a faint little nod.

As soon as the bus stopped, it was stormed by medics and medical volunteers. The woollies were gently escorted down the bus and onto stretchers. Romesh was hurried out, carried by two strong volunteers. The worst injured were given absolute priority. *Alec has his work cut out for him today in surgery,* I thought.

Ben, Nathan, Pearl, and I stayed behind to clean the bus, disinfect it from all the blood, puss, maggots and body fluids left behind, put the gear away, return the guns to the armoury for cleaning and oiling, in short, all the 'fun' stuff that was sure to kill any residue of euphoric joy from a successful mission. The team from the second bus were there, already hard at work disinfecting their vehicle. Bill walked over to congratulate our team for doing a good job under pressure. We chatted with him a bit about what we'd experienced. Luckily for Bill and Alpha Two, their guard wasn't quite as mountainous as Tony, and was easily disarmed. Suddenly Bill turned to me, pointing at my arm he said "That doesn't look too good, Sunny. You should go to the Medical Ward, have it sorted."

Now, suddenly, everyone's attention was on my arm.

"He's absolutely right, Sunny. It looks way worse now that I can see it in the light." Ben seemed truly concerned.

I wanted to say that I was fine. That it's nothing really, only a scratch. But suddenly the world started spinning, a bit more than usual.

"Whoa!" Ben caught me just before I tumbled to the floor. "I'm taking you to the Medical Ward right now."

"But… the bus…"

"It's OK. My team can help Nathan and Pearl when we finish ours," Bill said. "Go."

The medical ward was packed full of woollies and injured activists. Romesh was already in the operating theatre. Most woollies were in such a devastating state, I felt that me and my arm were just imposters here. Sanitation was a major issue, even with those slightly better off ones. *Were they ever made to feel like humans?* I wondered.

Medical volunteers were rushing between the beds, taking notes, hooking IVs, injecting Sleeping Gift, Antibiotics, all sort of concoctions. *There's so much work to be done here.* In the corner of my eye, further back in the room, my heart sank to notice Roth, busy assisting one of the volunteer nurses, hooking up a woollie to a plasma infusion. She briefly turned around, and for a passing moment our eyes met. Her eyes serious and focused, she wasn't smiling for a change. *Now THAT'S the face I remember.*

"Sunny!" I didn't quite manage to fully turn around before Rose was all over me, hugging and kissing me, her sweet perfume so at odds with everything I smelled that night.

"Rose! I'm so happy that your'e heeeeee…." The words didn't quite come, as my head was getting lighter, and breathing became a real effort.

"Sunny! Sunny!" I could hear Ben shouting to me through a thick screen of fogginess.

"I'm ffffffff…. ine…"

Please don't leave me here alone with Roth!

Lights out.

13.

That night, I finally had one of those crazy dreams, where things make no sense at all, but I just know there is a deeper meaning to them.

In my dream, I was lying in a hospital bed. It wasn't the bunker's Medical Ward, but more like the hospital where I first met Rose and Jonathan, after escaping the farm. I was lying still, without any ability to move my arms and legs. My head could only move a fraction. I tried to call for help, but no voice came out. Suddenly, a woman approached my bed. She looked menacing. I recognised her immediately, it was Jacqueline Roth, the way she looked at the farm. Her hair was short, with the fringe neatly combed to one side. She was wearing her white coat, a stethoscope hanging on her chest, in her hands she was holding a big syringe, with the most hideously long needle.

"Hello Sunny. I've been looking all over for you," she said. Her voice cold.

"Get away from me!" I tried to get up, to move, to scream, but my body didn't obey me.

She did not respond, only looked at me with great intent. Then suddenly, she smiled. One of her more recent Aunty Roth smiles.

"You murderer! You can't fool me! You're an evil woman! Get away from me!" My voice came out squeaky and small. I shook my head vehemently because nothing else in my body could move.

She leaned towards me, sticking me with the gigantic needle that seemed to go deeper and deeper into my arm. Her mouth was near my right ear, she was still smiling when she whispered, "nothing is as it seems."

14.

I woke up to see Ben by my bed.

"Hey…" He said quietly, "how are you? You gave us quite a scare!"

"What happened to me?" I wondered. My voice was croaky, but I could definitely move my limbs and be heard.

"It turned out that your wound was deeper than we thought," he said, his eyes soft. "And the ground where you skidded was probably more than a little filthy. Your wound was badly infected, and it went straight into your blood stream."

That sounded serious.

"They gave you four bags of blood, a ton of antibiotics… You were out for six whole days!" Then he raised his voice, sounding quite entertained, "even Romesh is recovering faster, eh buddy?" he chuckled, and I realised Romesh was my next bed roommate.

"Will be whooping your ass in a hundred meters sprint in no time," Romesh replied with a smile.

I raised my arm. It was bandaged. I was hooked up to an IV line.

"What are they pumping in me now?"

"Don't know. All sorts."

Memories of my odd dream lingered. "Was Roth anywhere near me?"

"Roth? Nah. Only Rose, also Alec and his team."

"Are you sure?"

"Sure, I'm sure, I was here the whole time. Well… almost."

"Really?" It made me so happy.

It was Romesh's turn to call out from his bed "Really, really. He was sleeping on a chair at your bedside and man, he snores. Don't marry him."

We all chuckled, then a short uncomfortable silence fell.

"Is Rose still here?" I wondered.

"She comes and goes, but she's here every day. I think she just left." Ben confirmed.

I looked around the room. It was far less occupied than when I came in. In fact, only two woollies were there, in the two beds opposite mine.

"Where is everyone? I wondered out loud.

"The sanctuary that is taking them has its own medical facilities, so those that were able to be transferred left a couple of days ago, after initial care, and… cleaning, obviously. Five are still in recovery. They'll be moved only when it's safe for them to do so. And… these two decided to stay here with us. To join us." He said and smiled at the occupants of the other two beds, both hooked up to IV lines, like me.

They smiled back. Little near-invisible smiles. Now, in the light, their skins were so pale, almost translucent. Their eyes, pale light grey, seemed almost colourless. Their faces were long, their noses pointy. Some freckles were scattered on their high cheekbones. Their hair was like nothing I've ever seen before. Its colour was hard to define, a bit sea-sand like. And it was rope-thick yet seemed soft and luxurious at the same time. They had it cut since coming here, it was much shorter now than on the night we rescued them. They looked so neat, scrubbed clean, in their clean clothes. Both laid in bed, their backs up right on the soft pillow, their long hands resting in their laps. They looked so incredibly alike; it was a bit like a visual illusion. *How will I ever be able to tell them apart?* I worried.

"Hi." I called to them.

They both looked at me a little blankly. The one to the right smiled a small-but-slightly-bigger-than-before smile. "Hello to you again."

Again. So, she might be the one from Building One. Possibly the brave one. Yes, it must be her.

"I'm Sunny," I waved my healthy arm at them.

"Good to know you, Sunny. My name is Venus," said the brave one. "This one is Ren," she indicated to the bed next to hers.

They had names. *Of-course* they had names. They were all individual people, why wouldn't they have names.

"Thanks for joining us, Venus, and Ren. Welcome." I smiled at them.

"You are the one to thank, Sunny. We thank to *you*. You saved us." The brave one said. Venus. She had a peculiar way of putting her words together, but I guessed that was just how they spoke, the woollies.

"It wasn't just me; it was all of us. But… you're welcome." I replied humbly. A wave of indescribable elation filled me. We did it. We saved lives. We gave them hope. We gave them a future.

"How many did we save, in the end?" I asked Ben.

"We got twenty-eight out," he said, not hiding his pride. "But…" his tone turned sombre, "we've lost two. One of them was from Bus Two. She was gone by the time they arrived here. She was too sick and malnourished. The other one was the wounded girl you rescued from room one, the last one you got out. She died a couple of days ago."

The wave of elation was replaced with deep, biting sorrow. Warm tears started streaming down my face.

Ben rushed to comfort me. "She was too far gone, Sunny. It's not your fault. Her wounds were horrific. Half her head was chopped off."

"I had her in my arms, Ben…" I cried, sobs of incontrollable grief shaking my body. "I had her in my arms…"

"I know." He said and reached for my hand.

"Maybe you can excuse me, Ms Sunny." Venus said calmly. "You talk about Loretta. She was my friend. You should not be crying. You gave to my friend three whole days to live. What we had before, that was not living, it was being dead but with breathing. You gave to her three days. For my friend Loretta, this was a miracle, what you gave to her."

I was deeply moved and grateful for those kind and thoughtful words. I couldn't tell how old Venus was. She may have been my age, or a bit older, but in some ways, she was certainly wiser.

15.

I felt like I'd only dozed off for a couple of minutes, but when I woke up, it was already morning. I was surprised to find Violet at my bedside.

"Good morning, Sunny," she greeted me with a smile. "I hope you don't mind that I sent Ben off to stretch his legs and take a shower."

"And thank goodness for that..." Romesh chuckled cynically from his bed.

"Oh, shut up, you." I giggled and tossed an extra pillow at him.

"Hey... I'm a disabled fella here!" He said, bemused, taking the pillow I threw and shoving it behind his back. "Not getting it back!"

"Excuse me, Mr Romesh," Venus surprised us all by joining the conversation. I loved her accent, the way she rolled her R's... RRRRRRRRomesh.... "But you will beg my pardon because I need to tell it to you, that *you* sir, are the one who snores in this room..." she smiled. A real, proper, big smile.

"That is a big fat lie..." he laughed.

"Well, I'm glad you're all keeping yourselves entertained," Violet interrupted. "What was it, erm, *Let Humour Be Thy Remedy* or something? I'm sure someone at some point in history said it."

I noticed that the bed next to Venus was empty. "Where's Ren?"

"Ms Ren has developed an addiction to hot showers. I believe she is trying to compensate for seventeen years in one week." Venus smiled, and I had to chuckle.

I was in awe of her. It was mesmerising to see how in just a few days of freedom, her individual personality has started to shine through. She was blossoming into the woman she was always meant to be, and I really liked her.

"So, how are you doing, Sunny?" Violet turned back to me.

"I'm feeling all right. When can I get out of here?"

"As soon as all your test results come back clear. Perhaps in a week or so."

A whole week? That was too long. I ached to get out of my bed and back to my life.

"I have something for you," she said and handed me a folded paper, "from Spirit."

I took it with sheer excitement but didn't open it. Not there, not in front of her. I'll read it to myself when she leaves.

"I've been thinking, why don't you go and spend a day at the beach house this weekend, if you're well enough, eh? Ben can drive you."

I was thrilled. "Yes, I'd love to go!"

"Wonderful. I'll let Rose know." She petted my hand, then added almost absentmindedly, "You did so well on the mission."

"Thank you."

"Now, get better. ALL of you." She said to no one in particular and left.

Excitedly, I opened the letter.

"Dear Sunny. I MISS YOU!!!!! Mum and Dad told me you got hurt when you were saving hair-slaves."

Mum and Dad. She called Rose and Jonathan Mum and Dad... It was strange, but I guess Spirit craved that kind of a relationship with them, from the very first day.

"I hope you'll get better fast because I'm worried and I miss you. When are you coming to visit us? It's been so long. Mum and Dad won't let me go to visit you, no matter how much I beg. They say some of the people in your hospital are hurt really badly. Did you like my necklace?"

The necklace! My hand reached for it, touching only bear skin. Where was it? I started to panic, when Venus called, "If you're looking for your necklace, Ms Sunny, It's there." Her long finger at the end of her long arm was pointing at the drawer chest between Romesh's bed and mine.

"Thank you." I smiled with relief, promptly tying it to my neck, then running my finger along the ripples and curves of the little shell.

"I can make a lot of things with the shells and twigs that we find on the beach. I'm also home schooled so I can do maths and dad says I'm the smartest one in the family. But you don't need to be jealous because you are by far the bravest one. Please come

visit me. Love, your sister, Spirit. XOXO (it means kisses and hugs)"

Sister… she called me her sister. I wasn't biologically related to Spirit, but I certainly felt like we were. Suddenly, deep pangs of homesickness overtook me. *Why have I waited so long to go and see them?* I was eager to go, right there and then, with the IV line still connected to me. Tears were starting to pool in my eyes when the weird sound of FFFFFt, FFFFFt, FFFFFt, FFFFFt, echoed through the corridor. Romesh and I exchanged puzzled looks. FFFFFt, FFFFFt, FFFFFt, FFFFFt, it was getting closer and closer. I eyed the drawer chest for something I could use to defend myself. I could tell Romesh was doing the same.

To my utter surprise, it was Ren. She walked into the room, smelling like an open shampoo bottle, her cheeks scrubbed bright red, a dark blue robe around her tall, slim body, a fluorescent-green towel tied tightly around her hair, dragging her feet in a pair of oversized, fluffy pink slippers. FFFFFt, FFFFFt, FFFFFt, FFFFFt, she walked to her bed and giggled.

16.

I remembered the first time I made my way to the beach house. Fresh out of the farm, already several terrifying encounters with Jacqueline Roth under my belt. In the car with Spirit, Jonathan and Rose, there was calmness and joy. We were making our way to true freedom. The car was warm. Spirit and I fell asleep. We listened to music, and then, awakened by the seaside, the smell of the ocean overwhelmed us. I'd never seen the ocean before that day. Grey, frothy and powerful, it was bewitching. I was captivated by the perpetual movement of the crushing waves. And here I was again, this time with Ben, making our way to the beach house. The narrow side road stretched on and on, until finally we saw it. The simple, yet beautiful house on the beach.

They were all waiting for us at the door. As soon as she saw us, Spirit began jumping up and down with excitement. Ben barely had a chance to park the car when she bolted towards us "Sunny! Sunny!"

I rushed out of the car, and she fell into my arms. She'd grown so much in the past year. Coming up to nine years now, her hair was long, her face wiser. She had more freckles, and she was so much taller.

"I missed you, Spirit." I said to her, my voice breaking with the overflow of emotions.

She looked up at me. "I missed you so much!" then quickly added "Wow, you look amazing, Sunny. Your hair is so shiny. And you're muscly!" She touched my arms, squeezing them a bit, and giggling.

"And you are taller and definitely cheekier!" I laughed.

Jonathan and Rose stepped out to greet us.

"You remember Ben, of course." I suddenly remembered I wasn't there alone.

"Of course," Rose smiled. "It is absolutely fantastic to have you both here." She then scanned the road leading to the house. "Best if you come inside."

Since the day Jacqueline Roth tried to kidnap me from this house, shooting Jonathan on her way in, then getting herself shot and captured by DaSLIF, the house was under constant surveillance and protection by our people. There was always a drone hovering over the area, and two activist cars were positioned strategically at all hours of the day, watching. But Rose was still nervous, and perhaps rightly so.

Walking inside, for the first time in over a year, the smell of home cooking, warm firewood and sea air filled me with longing. I missed this place.

A big piano was now the living room's centre stage, with abundance of framed photographs on it. Mostly of Spirit.

"I can play the piano!" she gushed and bolted towards the instrument, playing us a short, sweet tune, apologetically smiling at us when she made mistakes. We all clapped in the end, which made her decide to play us some more.

The house's large glass windows allowed the natural light and the beautiful view to flow uninterruptedly into the house. I walked to the large glass sliding doors that led to the deck, and the beach beyond it, and allowed the scenery to overtake me. Calmness seeped into every inch of my body. Suddenly, Jonathan decided to uncork a Champagne bottle. The cork popped with such a noise, that Ben and I instantly reached for our guns.

"Sorry, didn't mean to cause any trouble…" he said, bemused, as he poured the bubbly liquid into tall glasses. "A toast, eh?" he suggested, as he handed Spirit her glass of apple juice. "For you, young lady."

"So, what are we toasting then?" Jonathan asked.

"To family, to love, to activism, to total liberation!" I replied.

"Cheers!" came the choir of voices, followed by clicks of glasses.

I'd never had alcohol before. The Champagne was at the same time bitter and sweet, ticklish on the throat, and surprisingly nice. Innocent as it seemed, it immediately made me a little lightheaded, and instilled in me a sense of deep happiness.

Spirit took my hand and walked me through all the rooms, reintroducing me to the house I had already known. Jonathan did not exaggerate when he said that she filled their house with her art. Her colourful and happy creations were absolutely everywhere.

"I love your drawings, Spirit." I smiled.

She jumped with joy, "come take a look at this one!" There were two figures drawn childishly on a white sheet of paper, one taller than the other. One's hair was red, the other's dark brown. They were both smiling, holding their weird looking hands. "That's us!" She called. "You and me. Do you like it?"

"I love it!"

"I'll make a new one for you that you can take back with you."

"I love that idea." I kissed her on her head, realising how much closer to my face she had grown.

We sat on the deck under the large umbrella and had lunch together. The food was outstanding, and there was so much of it. Pasta, rice, potatoes, salads of vibrant colours, a mushroom pie and an onion pie (which Spirit helped to make, and was very proud of) some stewed cabbage, and fried artichokes. It was hard to fit it all in the stomach. The weather was nice and balmy, in spite of the sky being grey, and the conversations were relaxed. I quickly realised they were mostly interested in hearing about our trivial lives, not the missions. Not the dangers. The day-to-day routines. The way we spent our time each day, what we ate, who we socialised with, the number of times we cleaned the toilets. Spirit told us about being home schooled. Rose complimented her high mathematical skills. We talked about books. We talked about the weather. We talked about the ocean. We never said a word about our missions or Jacqueline Roth.

Time passed lazily, and when it was clear that no one was able to eat another morsel, Rose and Spirit cleared the table, then promptly brought out a delicious dessert of mango sorbet. Funny enough, we all found room in our tummies for that. As bowls were licked clean, Ben was quick to offer his help in the kitchen. He joined Rose and Jonathan inside, washing, and drying dishes, while I finally had some time alone with Spirit. She brought out some paper and felt-pens, and started drawing a picture for me to take. I watched her. She was the cutest little thing.

"So, how are you, Spirit?"

"I'm great." She was concentrating on her drawing.

"Do you get to play with children your age sometimes?"

"No, not really."

"Don't you get lonely, then? Sometimes?"

"I never had anyone to play with at The Farm either. I'm used to it."

That innocent little comment was hurting, because back then at the farm, I didn't pay her any attention at all. If she was lonely, and clearly, she was - I didn't notice and I didn't care. It was awful to think of this bright, sweet, brave girl alone and unloved.

"Besides," she added, "there is always something to do here. I'm never bored."

"I'm really happy to hear that, Spirit."

I watched her draw. She was now decorating her picture with love hearts. I couldn't help thinking, despite everything we had been through together, she was still just a little girl.

"You know, Spirit... before I left, you used to have nightmares at night... Do you still get them?"

"Not so much, only sometimes."

"What are they about, can you remember?"

Finally, she raised her head from the page. "Mostly it's about that night we spent over with those vile people, the Jessops. When I still have nightmares it's usually about the old man choking you to death. That I'm too late to get to you. Also, I sometimes dream about Rosichi and how she killed herself by touching the fence." She looked at me, her eyes full of innocence and wonder. "Do you still think of Rosichi sometimes?"

"Often." I confirmed. "I wonder what could have been if she didn't do it, you know... She would have had her baby by now... "I could sense my eyes tearing up fast.

"Oh, and sometimes I dream about that cruel White Suit woman who chased us everywhere and came here to kill Jonathan and Rose. I sometimes dream that she kills them," Spirit added.

I bit my tongue. I wanted to tell her about Jacqueline Roth but realised that adding to her worries wouldn't do Spirit any good.

"Do *you* still have nightmares?" she wondered.

"Oh, you bet. Often."

"What do you do?"

"What do you mean, Spirit?"

"When you have them? You're all alone, without us... is there anyone who can calm you down? Bring you some water?"

I felt the tears free-falling down my cheeks. "I have my friends... But you're right... it's hard without you."

"Friends like Ben?" She wondered.

"Yes."

Her eyes twinkled, "Do you love him?"

Oh boy, she was so cheeky! But in all honesty, that not-so-innocent question was the first time I'd been confronted about my emotions like that. Trust Spirit not to beat around the bush...

"I.... erm.... I..." I giggled uncomfortably and took a deep breath. "You know, I think I might..." I said and smiled. "Yes." Then, I winked at her and whispered, "but don't tell him!"

17.

It was late afternoon when Ben and I were back on the road. It was difficult to say goodbye to Spirit all over again, but this time I made her a promise to come and visit at least once every three months.

The skies were reddened with the promise of a nearing nightfall. The air was warm, the earth peaceful. It was such a perfect day. I was happy.

"Thank you for driving me," I said to Ben.

He grabbed my hand in one of his, leaving the other on the wheel. "It was totally my pleasure. I love your family. Don't ever ask anyone else to take you there but me…" he smiled warmly.

"I won't. I'm glad you came with me… I wanted you to come…" I felt the blush warming my face. Quickly I continued, "but I should learn how to drive, don't you think?"

"It's a very helpful skill to have." Ben agreed. "I can teach you, but only at night when it's safer for us."

"That would be amazing, when can we start?"

"Tomorrow?"

"Yes, please." *Could this day turn out any better?*

The road hazed with the lingering traces of a warm day, making the horizon seem a little smudgy. Ben and I were chatting happily when further ahead, on the side of the road, we could see what looked like a large truck. It was an odd sight. The truck seemed to be haphazardly parked, with part of it protruding into the road, semi-blocking one traffic lane of the already quite narrow road. Out of the ordinary sights like that were always ill-boding to people like us. Anything could be a trap; anything could spell danger. As we got near, Ben slowed down. We drove past the truck at near-walking speed. I grabbed my gun in my hands. All the truck's wheels seemed to be fine, there was no clear puncture in any of them. I looked through the narrow slits that pierced the truck along its side. It was dark inside. Suddenly, in a terrifying split second, I could see!

"EYES!"

"What?"

"EYES! Eyes in the truck!"

"What do you mean?"

"Eyes in the truck! Stop the car!"

Ben sped up and pulled over in front of the large vehicle. I bolted out through my door. There was no one in the cabin. It seemed to be abandoned. I rushed over to the side of the truck. A strong smell of faeces and urine emanated from it. I gaped through the nearest slit. It was rimmed with filth all around. *Where were the eyes?*

WOOOFT! A hand pushed through the narrow slit, smacking my nose. I took a couple of steps back, rubbing my face. *What is this?* But the hand was left there, hanging, reaching out of the truck, its palm open, begging.

Hesitantly, I got closer again. I peaked in through a different slit. The truck was full. Countless pairs of fearful eyes were staring at me.

Someone else stuck their hand through a slit. "Help ussss!" said the hand. "Waterrrrr…"

"Waterrrrr…. Waterrrr…." The truck hummed suddenly in a faint choir of desperate voices. "Waterrrr…"

I ran back to the car. "Ben, the truck is full of people. We have to help them!"

Realising that this was not just a short snooping-around stopover, Ben switched the engine off and joined me. "Bring your water!" I called back at him, already in a hurry to return to the hand.

By now, the side of the truck was adorned with tens of stretched hands, reaching out through every slit. I put some water in a palm. The hand's owner pushed her way through to get her face as close to the slit as possible, cupping the hand to her lips, loudly sucking every drop.

"Waterrr… waterrr….. Help ussssss!..."

I jumped from hand to hand, pouring a bit of water in each, then going back and pouring more.

Ben was near me now, watering hands with his own bottle. Something in this scene was desperate and hopeless.

"Ben, we have to save them." I shouted, my voice shaking. "We need to take this truck!"

"What? How?"

"You can drive!"

"I can drive a car…"

"How different can it be?"

"Very different."

"Then…" I gave it a frantic thought. I looked up to the sky. Surely there was a drone following us all the way from the beach house. They could see us. I knew they could.

"Call Omega. Tell Omega to send a bus!"

"Sunny…." Ben was hesitant. "I know why you want to do it, but it's… it's not a chartered mission…"

"Who gives a shit?" *Did I just say that?* "So, it's not a chartered mission! But there are people here, and they're obviously dying, Ben. We *must* save them."

He looked at me, then something in his eyes clicked. "You're absolutely right. I'm on it."

As he returned to the car, I kept watering the begging hands. There were so many. Soon enough I ran out of water. "Waterrrr…. Waterrrr…." The hands kept pleading. "I'm sorry…" I whispered in utter despair. "I have no more…"

"Waterrrr…. Waterrrr…."

I leaned my head against the truck. "I have no more water," I said in despair, "I'm sorry."

"Oi! What'cha think you're doing there! Get away from my truck!" A man came running out of the shrubs by the roadside. He was bold and round, slightly elderly, rather unkempt. Holding a toilet paper roll in one hand and a worn out scruffy old magazine in the other. *Well, now we know why the truck was abandoned.*

"Get away from there!" the man rushed towards me.

"Is this your truck?" *I must delay him.*

"Yes, it's my truck. Move away. What'cha doing anyway?"

"I was giving them some water."

"What'cha want to waste your water on these ones? They're as good as dead."

"Where are you taking them?"

"Are you dim? To the Freeze works."

"What's that?" *Please don't go.*

"The slaughterhouse! What'cha stupid or somt'n?"

"But why?"

"Lady, are you messin' with me or somt'n? This is food. People wanna eat."

"But it's not food! Look at them! It's NOT FOOD! What's the difference between you and them?"

"Lady, I wasn't bred to be eaten. So, no Miss, it ain't like me. Now git." He was pacing back towards the cabin. *No, no. no. you can't drive away.*

"Hey mister!" I called to him. The man turned around, clearly agitated. "Look how scared they are! Don't you care? Don't you care that they're scared and that… they don't want to die!"

"Miss, I don't know what cave you just climbed out of. I'm just doing my job. Now move your car out of my way or I'll ram it." My brain was desperately searching for something else to say that would keep him engaged. He was about to turn and climb the high steps to the driver's cabin.

"Hey Mister! Mister!"

One of his feet was already on the first step. Very reluctantly he put his leg back on the road and looked back at me.

"What's your name?" *Lame!*

"It ain't your fucking business!" He said and was about to climb up to the cabin, when Ben appeared behind him like a ghost, and smacked him on the head with the heel of his gun.

The man fell to the ground, unconscious. Ben searched his pockets, his driver's licence showed that his name was Larry.

"Sorry, Larry." Ben whispered. "You'll have a nasty headache in the morning."

It was hard work, heaving Larry back into the truck, with Ben pulling him up from the inside of the cabin by his torso, and my pushing his legs from the road underneath his heavy body. Eventually, Larry was laid comfortably across the two front seats. We placed some masking tape on his mouth and tied his hands together, as a precaution. When finished, Ben and I were both sweating profusely.

"You're crazy." Ben looked at me, breathing heavily, and smiled. "In a good way."

"Are they sending someone?"

"Yes. Nathan is bringing a bus."

We waited by the truck with our guns drawn. Ben stood at the front, near our car, while I guarded from the back. "Help usssss.... Help usssss...." The choir went on, but slower and quieter, as energy drained from the victims inside.

Night was falling fast. A pair of headlights could be seen far in the horizon. I smiled. *Finally! The bus is here!* But joy turned to cold fear when the lights turned out to be a police car.

"Ben!" I called to him in terror.

"I see it." He confirmed, his voice filled with worry. "Leave it to me."

The police car slowed as it passed us. The officer lowered his window, taking in the odd scene, sternly looking at Ben, as he kept driving. I quickly sneaked behind the truck, not sure if he'd noticed me. The police car kept going, and momentarily I breathed easy, only to realise it was turning around, coming back towards us the other way. I stayed behind the truck, trying desperately not to be seen. Again, the officer drove very slowly, menacingly, observing Ben via the rolled down window. He stopped his car next to Ben.

"Good evening officer," Ben said, attempting to sound casual. His gun was back in its holster.

"What's going on here, son?"

"Nothing officer, my friend had a puncture, so we're helping him replace the tyre."

"Where's your friend?"

"Oh, he just went to the bushes to take a… you know… nature called…"

"He's taking a crap and you're changing his tyre?" The officer sounded puzzled.

"Yeah, when you gotta go…" Ben tried his best, but he wasn't doing a very good job at convincing the officer this unusual scene was benign. The officer drove a few meters on and parked his car just ahead of ours. My heart was beating so fast, I could feel it bursting out of my chest. Slowly, almost reluctantly, the officer hurled himself out of his car. He wasn't a young man and didn't seem happy to be troubled by whatever was going on. Purposefully, he walked over to Ben, "Now what tyre is the one in trouble?" he asked. Ben waffled something incoherent. "I didn't get that, son. Which one is it?"

"Erm… that one there… in the back…"

"Show me," the officer said. He was not kidding around.

Ben had little choice but to lead the officer to the back of the truck. He was deliberately slow, the officer pacing behind him. Each slow step decidedly bringing them closer to me. My mind was racing. *What do I do? What do I do? What do I do?* As they moved towards me, crouching around the back of the truck, my only instinct was to try and remain hidden. As they moved, so did I, stealthily sneaking around the truck, away from them. As quietly as possible, I circled the truck in the opposite direction, going around the cabin, and out the other side. Technically, I was now behind them.

"This tyre seems to be just fine, son," the officer said.

"Erm, yes, we already replaced the punctured one," Ben kept improvising.

"Where did you put the other tyre?" The officer pressed on. He wasn't buying it.

"We... erm... I ...." Ben was struggling.

"Are you going to keep shitting me, boy?" The officer asked, his voice harsh. "What's going on here?"

Ben hesitated. I could hear his feet shuffling uncomfortably, stressfully, on the ground.

"Son, please follow me back to my car," the officer instructed Ben. He was about to turn around.

Oh no, that was bad. Bad. Bad. Bad. The officer would call for reinforcement. He'll arrest Ben. He'll find me... He'll send me back to Natures... These victims would remain in the truck and be slaughtered.... What do I do? What do I do?

There was but a second to decide and another second to act. There was really nothing I could do. Nothing, except...

WHACK.

Before the police officer had the chance to turn around, I sneaked from behind and hit him on the back of his head with the heel of my gun. *It worked with Larry...* He fell to the ground. I took a good look at him. He had a large, grey moustache and round, kind face. I felt sorry for having to do that. In all truth, things felt like they were getting a bit out of hand.

"Shit happens when it's not a chartered mission." Ben said, "you did the only thing you could do."

We carried the officer back to his car and laid him there. We did not bind him.

"In truth, shit happens also when it *is* a chartered mission." Ben said, as we closed the police officer in his car. "It just happens all the time, because total liberation is illegal and slave exploitation is everywhere." He took a deep breath. "You know, our faces will now be plastered in all police units and all stations. You and me just earned our place on the Most Wanted List."

I nodded. I've been there before, of course, when I escaped the farm.

"And that probably means no driving lessons for a while. Possibly no beach house for a while either. Violet won't let us out of the bunker until it all calms down."

He was right, of course, but that meant that I had just lied to Spirit, and it hurt.

Finally, Nathan appeared with the bus. He parked behind the truck and came over to Ben and me, waiting by the police officer's car, just in case he woke.

It was a strange scene to behold: the bus, the truck, our car, and the police car, all parked awkwardly on the side of a lonely road.

Nathan unbolted the truck's back doors and shined his flashlight in.

A sticky huddle of women and children looked back at us. They were all in tatters, filthy from head to toe, their eyes red, their lips cracked. *How long since they had been given any food or drink?* The children in particular, looked completely emaciated. Slowly and carefully, we offloaded them from the truck and onto the bus. Fifty-five lives in total.

I stayed with them in the bus, while Ben drove the car behind us. The survivors were silent. I was silent. Nathan was silent. I knew that once we arrived at the bunker, I'd have to face the full wrath of Violet's anger. This was an unchartered mission, for which I risked myself, I risked Ben, Nathan and all of us. *I bet I'll be punished. Maybe I won't be allowed on missions anymore.*

Nathan drove fast, much faster than he'd normally drive. We had to get away from the police officer in case he woke up and alerted the entire police force. I was awash with very strong contradicting emotions. On the one hand, utter joy at saving these women and children, and on the other, the deepest sense of guilt for doing it so unprofessionally, on a whim.

We arrived at the bunker, the bus was lowered in. Alec was there with his assistant Billie and a few volunteers, to help the survivors into the Medical Ward. Slowly they disembarked the bus; Women, children, some as young as Spirit, huddled together, so full of fear. Nathan jumped off the bus and onto the platform. "She's waiting for you," he said. I nodded.

Violet and Peter were both in the Command Room, both looking very unhappy. I walked in, my head lowered in shame.

"Take a seat, Sunny." Violet said, her voice firm but not unkind.

I sat myself on one of the chairs, braced for the scolding.

"We'll be talking to Ben as well, but I wanted to see you first," she paused, looking sternly at me. "There's a good reason we do not engage in unchartered missions," she said. "Even with chartered missions it is hard to control all the elements and stay out of danger, so with unchartered ones, the chances that things might go wrong are much higher, and with potentially catastrophic consequences!" She sighed. "What if you had us exposed, Sunny? Risking all of us, all the future missions? What if they had caught you? What if you were killed?" She stopped to let her words sink in. "I know what motivated you to help. I know how hard you wanted to save these women and children. I understand. You did what many of us would be too scared to do, even as activists. Your bravery puts us all to shame..." *Did she just... compliment me?* "For you, Sunny, total liberation is not just a slogan, and I admire that. But you must always think before you act. We never mess with the police. Ever. It's the worst thing that you could do. You get on the wrong foot with the police, and within a month all our operations are toast, our volunteers thrown in jail. Do you *really* want to be a fugitive again, Sunny?" I shook my head. Of course not. She paused. "As it turns out, poor Sammy is a friend of ours." *Wait, what?* "You had no way of knowing it, obviously, and you did the only thing that you thought you could do. But he was probably only having a bit of a laugh at your expense, being all macho, inspecting the scene. He's been helping us for years. It will take a good bottle of whiskey and a nice basket of chocolates to smooth this one though…"

I looked at her, bewildered. "So… am I off the hook?"

"You were never *on* the hook, Sunny. I don't even know how to begin to hook you…" She smiled. "But I need you to understand, we are all here to do the right thing. Don't risk it. Don't risk us. Only people like us can bring the change you wish to see in the world."

I still wasn't sure what was going on. Was I not to get punished?

"Come," Peter urged me. "Your friends have something to say about what just happened."

Oh, I see what they were doing. It's a group punishment.

Peter led me to the Community Room. I walked behind him, preparing myself for anything that could happen in there. In my head I was going over all the possible arguments I could use to refute their angry charges. *I didn't really put them in danger. Nothing really happened… Fifty-five lives were saved…* But once I walked in, I realised I was not at all prepared for what awaited me.

They were all clapping.

18.

I was tired. It had been a long and emotional day. I spent three hours in the Medical Ward, helping the team to triage and treat our newly liberated slaves. Most of them were severely dehydrated, one child showed signs of pneumonia. They were all very fatigued. Mattresses were laid on the floor as there were not enough beds to accommodate them all. We offered them medicated water followed by some fruit juice, but nothing to eat. Food had to be administered very carefully because of the risk of metabolic disturbance, which could cause death. They didn't talk to us, or to each other, so tired and overwhelmed they were.

It was past midnight when I finally made my way to my room. My body was aching for some sleep. I sneaked in quietly, not to wake Pearl up. She was one of the loudest to congratulate me for the day's achievement, but she might be even louder to reprimand me if I dared to wake her. Pearl loved her sleep. In silence I slipped into my pyjamas and was about to brush my teeth when a short rap on the door made me jump. I opened the door to see Ben, standing outside my room, a little bashful.

"Hey," I said.

"Hey," he smiled. "What a day, eh?"

"Yeah…"

"You, erm, you left this in the car," he said, and handed me Spirit's picture, the one she made for me that morning.

"Thank you." I nearly forgot about it, but now that I had it back, I was relieved.

Ben hesitated. I sensed he was about to say something else, but I beat him to it.

"I apologise," I said.

"What for?" He looked genuinely surprised.

"For forcing you into the position of having to help me. For putting you in danger."

He smiled. "There is nothing you need to apologise for. If anything, it's me who should apologise to you!"

"What for?"

"For not thinking about liberating these people myself, for not thinking on my feet fast enough…"

"I… I thought you were a little angry with me, you know?" I said honestly.

"Angry? Sunny, you are way off…. I'm angry with myself not you… I'm not used to doing my best with unchartered missions… but… I guess… life with you *is* an unchartered mission, isn't it?" He smiled, a little nervously, "And I want it… I want life with you…."

My jaw dropped a little. *Was he just saying what I thought he was saying?*

"If you want to, that is" he was quick to add.

I nodded, still a bit stunned. My breath was rapid, my heart beating fast.

He leaned towards me and kissed me lightly on the lips. "Awesome," he smiled.

I smiled back, suddenly losing all capability of speaking.

"I love you, Sunny." He whispered, and kissed me again, his lips soft and warm and wanting. Bolts of electricity were shooting uncontrollably through my body. The taste of him energised me, the feel of him... *What's happening to me?*

"Oi, lovebirds!" Pearl's yell from the room made us both jump. "Can you two please *not* smooch each other by the door when I'm trying to sleep?"

We giggled.

"Well... good night then..." He smiled.

I waved to him as he left, still unable to utter a word.

Eighteen Months since Joining DaSLiF

19.

Six months had gone by since liberating the bus full of victims on their way to be slaughtered. They stayed with us in the bunker for three weeks, until places for all of them were secured in various sanctuaries. In small groups they were evacuated to these places of hope and compassion, until none were left. Ben and I made our relationship public knowledge, though no one at all was taken by surprise. Once or twice a week, based on our free time and availability, we ventured out with one of the cars, as he taught me how to drive. I was amazed at how exciting I found driving to be, and the utter sense of freedom it provided. I developed quite a thirst for speed, which wasn't exactly to Ben's liking, but he had to agree that I showed the necessary confidence. The problem was always going to be that I could not be issued with a formal licence. For the world I was - and always would be - a dairy slave. Women like me were nothing but tools, we were not issued licences. Not having a licence meant that no matter how good a driver I was, I could not be assigned as the designated driver on chartered missions. Risk minimisation was always the primary requirement, and being caught driving without one, on a night of a rescue mission, could jeopardise it all. I knew that from the start, but I still went out eagerly with Ben on these nightly lessons. If nothing else came out of it, at least it gave us some time alone away from the bunker.

I kept my promise to Spirit and visited her twice in the next six months. I drove Ben and me to the beach house early in the morning, and Ben drove us on the way back. The days spent at the beach house were perfect droplets of sanity and calm, ones that we would savour once the madness of planning our next missions picked up again.

The romantic relationship with Ben was a fantastic escape from obsessively thinking about Jacqueline Roth. Having something new to focus on, that filled my life with excitement and anticipation, left very little time for dwelling on fears and worries. Now and then I ran into her when I was by myself, still trying to avoid contact, remaining cordial yet distant.

While I was perfecting my driving skills, Venus and Ren were immersing themselves with activists' training. It turned out they sucked at pretty much anything but drone operating. Something about being the Eye in the Sky appealed to their unique sense of silent communication. They mastered it so quickly, soon they started implementing improvements to the machines themselves. No one could figure out or explain how they knew what they were doing, with no applicable education or knowledge, but soon enough all drones were able to communicate with each other, and record sound, not just images. This was a huge step forward, which also meant that on all missions from now on, Venus and Ren were the unrefuted Eye in the Sky operators.

Before long, enough time had passed since the previous chartered mission. It was time to go out and liberate some more.

20.

For the next mission, my name was called as a core planning member.

The long, oval table in the Board Room was no longer foreign to me. I knew the routine, I knew the people, I no longer felt like an imposter playing at the big kids' playground. I belonged.

"Our next mission," Violet announced and pressed the buttons on the wall, immediately presenting the sky map of our new destination. "Is going to be... welcome Nathan... is going to be... an underground Fight Club!"

Murmurs of excitement and approval. *What's an underground Fight Club?*

"To those who are unfamiliar with the concept of a fight club," she read my mind, "it is a particularly cruel place of entertainment where fighting to the death takes place between two participants, while bets are placed on the potential winner. In this case, the players are young men, stolen or kidnapped from their homes as young children. For years they are tortured and made into ruthless killing machines by being fed a diet of testosterone, methamphetamines, and adrenaline. Otherwise, they are control-starved and sadistically abused, which to my knowledge includes being raped. Their teeth are filed to be razor sharp. They are released into the ring naked, with nothing but their teeth as weapons. Only one of them is allowed to come out alive. People bet enormous amounts of money on who'd win. Basically, the two bite and tear each other to bits. It's one of the more gruesome and barbaric things you can imagine."

The description alone made me feel ill.

Violet changed the sky map to show images of some of these men. The images were horrid. They didn't even look like humans anymore. They were demonic creatures, their eyes mad. Sharp, knife-like teeth, dripping blood.

"These men are beyond saving. No sanctuary would accept them. Too violent and unpredictable. Unfortunately, there's too little experience with successfully rehabilitating them."

She swapped the images back to the map.

"Our aim, in this case, is to rescue the baits."

Baits?

"These men need to train, hone their viciousness, perfect their killer's instinct. They don't train on each other, it's a waste of money. No… they train with baits. Young, kidnapped boys who are perceived as weak, soft, unwilling. Instead of making them into fighters, they throw them to the ring. Live baits. They're instantly killed, of course, but with much suffering, and unimaginable fear." Violet paused and gulped some water from her glass. This was rough, even on her. "They're only children…" She said, her voice a little shaky. "Some are no older than four or five years old."

Around the table people were visibly shocked. I swallowed hard. I thought I've already seen the worst of what humans were capable of, but I guess I was wrong. Humanity could stoop so much lower still.

"This little establishment is completely illegal, but nothing's being done about it, because even high-ranking police officers, politicians, businessmen and social leaders quench their thirst for raw entertainment there. Apparently, some of the owners at the very top of Natures Farms spend their money there. It was Jacqueline Roth's idea we target it."

That last comment took me by surprise. How I wished I could have sniggered at her 'contribution' to the liberation effort... but saving these boys – it was a brilliant idea.

"The fighting men are kept here," She pointed to a square building adjacent to the main ring. "Each is kept chained in their own tiny cell. No outside communication at all. There are thirty of them in this establishment at the moment, in total, but since death and mutilation are so frequent, more and more are brought in all the time. It's impossible to trace all the shitholes they are brought in from. Could be anywhere, any backyard." She sighed. "The baits are kept here," she pointed to a smaller building, also adjacent to the ring, but on the other side of it. "There's a trap door leading from the ring to this room, where the baits are kept. I don't know who chooses which one is about to be served as bait. Maybe it's the operators, but we must be prepared for the possibility it's the fighter himself, by having access into this little room from the ring. It's a risk."

"How many baits are there now?" Suli queried.

"Excellent question, Suli. We're not sure. We believe between thirty and fifty."

There was a stunned silence around the table. Most of us were already pretty accustomed to seeing horrendous cruelty inflicted as part of the food industry. But these horrors were perpetuated for sheer entertainment and betting thrills. It was indescribable.

"Also, our aim is to destroy the bank. They have a lot of cash on site, and keep it in this building here," she pointed with her purple marker. "We're going to blow it up."

Violet opened the floor for questions, comments, and planning suggestions. My only contribution, to Miley's delight, was that we needed heavy snipers' protection.

After several hours of meticulous discussions, the hatched plan was this:

Alpha One, led by Ben, included me, Pearl, Nathan, Bill, George, Simon, and Joshua. Our task was dedicated to breaking into the Baits' cell from the outside and pulling them out to safety.

Alpha Two, led by Andy, were in charge of blowing up the bank.

The Red Eyes, or snipers' team, led by Miley, included four other sharp shooters, to protect us from each corner.

Our Eyes in the Sky operators were Venus and Ren.

"One last thing," Violet added before we scattered off, "You should know that Jacqueline Roth is going to be in the Command Room with us during the mission. She'd been in this Fight Club facility before, it might help us."

Somehow, that bit of information didn't put my mind at ease. Betting on this vile activity is exactly what the Jacqueline Roth I remembered would do. I wasn't confident she wouldn't again.

Now all we needed to do was start preparing.

21.

Exciting and terrifying as it was, the nearing mission was not the only thing that kept my mind occupied. There was another mission on my mind... Ben. It was around that time when suddenly, I simply couldn't stop thinking about him. It was hard to concentrate on the task ahead when my mind was full of Ben... His eyes. His hands. His soft lips. His hair. The way he put his hand through his hair. The little scar just above his right eyebrow. His smile. His little dimple, just on one side. The place where his neck met his shoulder. That little crevice above the collarbone. His chest. His abdomen. The thin trail of dark hair that led from his navel down, down, into his pants... I couldn't get my mind off that trail of hair... or off Ben's pants. It was as if I was possessed by madness which completely took over me. There was a yearning, almost to the point of physical pain. We never really had much time alone, though, and the little we had was always on public territory, which meant that all this *need* remained blocked in my head. In public, I was quite embarrassed about displaying strong emotions towards him. Holding hands was the most I agreed to when there were other people around. Even the odd hug made me uncomfortable. But what I really wanted, was to get Ben alone... in private.

It was just another morning after a night of mission prep that Venus approached me on my way to the gym. I knew it was her and not Ren. Since they had been with us for a while now, I had realised they weren't *that* identical. Their freckles pattern, for example, was completely different. Venus had more freckles, and they were thicker together, slightly of darker shade, and unlike Ren, she had some on her nose. She was also a smidgen taller.

"Have you been naughty Ms Sunny?" she asked with a twinkle in her pale eyes.

"Huh?"

"Violet asked to see you…"

"Oh… What for?"

"I don't know… She's waiting for you… in the Medical Ward."

The Medical Ward? That was strange. I quickly made my way there, wondering what it was that I'd done this time. Violet was waiting for me in one of the consultation rooms. She looked relaxed, even amused.

"Hi Sunny, thanks for coming. Sorry for the short notice."

I walked in and took a seat, still unclear what it was all about.

"So, how is it going with you and Ben?"

Huh? "Great."

"You two seem very cosy together," she said and cleared her throat, then continued matter-of-factly, "I'll just get straight to the point. I wanted to talk to you about sex."

Oh.

"We don't have a policy against people hooking up with each other here. You are all now above the age of consent, and we don't feel it's our right to interfere with that aspect of your lives."

I still couldn't quite believe that we were having that conversation.

"But what we do insist on, is that you are aware of what you're doing and are taking the necessary precautions." She paused and looked at me carefully. "Especially you, Sunny."

"Me?"

"Yes. You must realise that you were designed as a breeder. Everything in your body has been manipulated for easy conception, smooth pregnancy, and maximum breastmilk yield. I'm sorry to be so blunt, but this is just how it is."

I must have looked stunned because I was.

"So, unless you want to become a mother soon, you must use protection."

I nodded.

"If you've done it already, don't be alarmed. I asked Billie to give you a thorough check-up." I looked at her, still in a state of shock.

"Have you? Done it?"

"What?"

"Sex. Did you already have sex?"

"No!"

This was so much worse than the conversation I had with my mother about getting the monthly bleeding.

"Good then, we have one less thing to worry about. Still, Billie will check you and provide you with contraception. Oh, and by the way, Alec is having the same conversation with Ben, so please don't think we expect you to assume all the responsibility."

Alec was talking to Ben about having sex with me? That's just great.

"It's Ok, Sunny, everyone gets this little pep talk at some point here." She smiled.

*

Armed with contraception and advice, having been probed and poked and looked at from every possible angle, I felt my desire had cooled off somewhat. Maybe that was the whole purpose of it, who knows? Somehow, I was embarrassed to tell Ben about it, and managed to successfully avoid him the whole day. But I couldn't avoid Pearl.

"What was it about?"

"Nothing important."

"What're all these pills?"

"Erm… I'm supposed to take them now. Billie gave them to me."

"You had the SEX talk!!! I knew it!"

I felt my cheeks redden and my mouth go dry. Pearl giggled. "Did you do it?"

"What?"

"Have sex with Ben? Did you do it?"

"No!"

"Liar."

"I'm not lying. Did *you?*"

"Did I what? Have sex with Ben?" she asked with a slightly horrified tone.

"No, have sex… with someone."

"No."

"How come?"

Pearl rolled her eyes. She didn't respond.

"Romesh is handsome…"

"I'm not into Romesh."

"What about Bryan, then? I see him looking at you sometimes at mealtimes."

"I'm not into Bryan, and anyway, it's not me he looks at, it's Nathan."

Oh. "What about A…"

Pearl interrupted me, agitated, "Sunny, I'm not into any of them, OK? I'm not into boys!"

Oh… How did I not notice that? What sort of a friend am I? A bad one.

After a short, shamed silence I said "What about Miley? She's cute."

"Sunny?"

"Yes?"

"Stop."

"OK."

22.

Ben and I had all the knowledge and protection, but not a single opportunity to put what we'd learned into practice. Our relationship maintained itself on our strong friendship, snogging here and there, and mental intimacy.

Meanwhile the mission was drawing closer. Excitement levels were steadily rising, so when people began to feel a bit achy, most of us thought nothing of it. It was when people started falling like flies with flu symptoms that everyone realised, we had an outbreak.

It's easy to assume that being isolated from the world as we were, meant that viruses and diseases did not affect us. The truth was, that we weren't quite as isolated as you'd think. People who had supportive families nearby still went out to meet them, just like Ben and I would visit the beach house. Food still had to be sourced from growers, and day-to-day supplies from suppliers. We'd had survivors staying in the Medical Ward twice in the previous eight months, some of them were very ill. The opportunities to bring in diseases were always abundant. The problem with living in the bunker, where air was circulated and inhaled over and over again, was that regardless of all the heavy filters, once inside, diseases were hard to avoid.

This flu came into the bunker like a silent assailant. One by one people succumbed. After only five days since it first hit, the kitchen at mealtimes was nearly empty, and the Medical Ward completely full. Some, like Pearl and me, were affected only lightly, in and out of the ward within three days. We were told we had natural immunity, possibly due to the fact we both grew up on Natures Farm and were bred to survive. Some, like Nathan, were more severely affected. Their bodies took longer to develop immunity and fight off the disease. They stayed at the ward for up to ten days, achy and sick, but still lucid. And others, like Ben, were completely consumed by it, their bodies struggling to cope, and had to be heavily sedated and monitored, while strong medication was pumped into their veins. I was eaten alive with worry. *What if I lose him? I can't lose him.* It was beyond comprehension to lose Ben to some silly, mundane disease, when the real danger was supposed to be awaiting us outside. I stayed by his bed continuously, so troubled, I couldn't read or engage in any other bedside activity. I'd just sit there and watch him. I could concentrate on absolutely nothing else. For hours I'd sponge his boiling body with a cool cloth, brush his hair, hold his hands. *Wake up Ben.* Slowly, the ward was cleared out of the recovered. Only Ben and Leah remained. I was so burdened with worry, I couldn't even care much about seeing Jacqueline Roth there, helping to look after Leah.

After almost two weeks, Ben's body started responding to the drugs. His breathing began to ease, his temperature started to come down. Relief was sweet and so welcome. One afternoon, after careful checks, Alec removed the tube that was helping him breathe, and weaned him off the sedatives. Slowly Ben awoke. He was weak, dizzy, and disoriented, but he was well and truly out of danger.

"Hey," he croaked my way.

"Hey," I leaned over, my hand cupping his face gently. "Welcome back to me, Ben."

"I had the craziest dreams…"

I smiled. I knew a thing or two about crazy dreams.

I stayed by his bedside as he slowly recovered. His body was stripped of its strength and energy. He still suffered from strong occasional muscle aches and ate very little. To ease up his recovery, Alec suggested Ben receive the Sleeping Gift once a day, as he found it hard to sleep, and sleep was vital for his recovery. I helped administer the drug, making sure he was comfortable and relaxed before I kissed him goodbye and sent him off to Dreamland. The timed forced sleep seemed to be helping him. His appetite grew and so did his vitality. It was during my third week in the ward with Ben that I left him for a few moments to take a shower. I had hardly washed or looked after myself at all in the past three weeks. I had plenty of offers from friends to replace me, so I could go and refresh, but I refused to leave Ben. In the last couple of days, with Ben making some real progress and sleeping soundly due to the Sleeping Gift, I allowed myself to go and wash, change my smelly clothes, and stretch my legs. On one particular afternoon, I allowed myself to take a longer shower, washed my hair and even indulged in applying some moisturiser to my skin. Lazily, my hair still damp, I made my way back to the ward, knowing that Ben would still be sleeping, so there was no rush.

The corridor was dimly lit and quiet, I was deep in my thoughts as I approached the door.

At the entrance to the large room, my eyes nearly popped out of their sockets. I felt like someone had just punched my stomach full force and ripped my lungs out of my chest.

What the heck? WHAT. THE. HECK?

In full view, Jacqueline Roth was standing at Ben's bed. She was holding a syringe in her hand. The syringe was full. She was about to inject something into his bloodstream. In horror, I glimpsed at her, trying to comprehend the scene unfolding. Her face was severe and emotionless, none of those phony smiles. Finally, it was the Jacqueline Roth I was much more familiar with. The woman who murdered my mother, shot Jonathan, tried to kill Rose, wanted to enslave me. The Jacqueline Roth of my nightmares.

"GET AWAY FROM HIM!" I screamed at her with the full ferocity of my shock.

She jumped back and dropped the syringe on the floor.

I leaped at her, my brain in overdrive with guilt, surprise, and raw anger. I only meant to push her away from his bed, but in effect I practically threw her crashing on the floor.

"WHAT WERE YOU DOING?" my voice was shaky, deep, full of venom.

Jacqueline Roth, still on the floor, was whimpering something incomprehensible.

"WHAT WERE YOU GIVING HIM?"

"I... I.... I'm sorry, I..."

"SPEAK!" I was screaming at her, my head so full of pumped blood I was getting dizzy.

"It's... I... I was giving him the Sleeping Gift, that's all... Just a

Sleeping Gift. Here," she reached for the syringe on the floor, "see for yourself." Her hand shook as she handed it to me.

I grabbed the syringe, not bothering to look at the sticker.

"YOU WERE TRYING TO KILL HIM!"

"What? No… no… Sunny, no. I was only trying to help…"

"BUT I JUST GAVE HIM THE DRUG AN HOUR AGO! YOU WERE OVERDOSING HIM!"

"I… I'm so sorry, I didn't know…"

"What do you MEAN you didn't know? I BLIMMIN' CHARTED IT!" I shouted, shoving the medicine chart in her face. "RIGHT HERE!"

"I'm so sorry, I'm so sorry… I forgot to check…"

"SAVE IT," I screamed and pressed the emergency button.

In less than a minute, Violet, Alec, and Billie came running into the room.

"What happened?" Violet asked, panting, her eyes on Jacqueline Roth, still on the floor.

"She was trying to kill Ben! I caught her!"

Violet's face was suddenly ashen with shock. "What?"

"It was a mistake… a mistake… I'm so sorry…" Roth said, whimpering and shaking.

"She was overdosing him with the Sleeping Gift. I only gave him a dose an hour ago, and I charted it!"

Violet picked up the medicine chart and read it with scrutiny.

"Jacqueline?" She asked the woman on the floor.

"I forgot to check... I thought I was being helpful... I'm so sorry.... I'm so sorry!" She started to cry.

Violet seemed torn.

"Violet. She was killing him!" I pressed on.

"It was a mistake... I'm sorry!" Roth kept begging.

"I'm sorry, Jacqueline...." *Yes! Kick her out!...* "But I'll need to use the Truth Serum on you once again. The whole situation does look very suspicious."

Roth nodded, still whimpering, drying her tears. She got up from the floor and followed Violet out of the room.

"What's a Truth Serum?" I asked Billie.

"It's a drug that makes it very hard for someone to lie while confronted with direct questions."

"What do you mean by very hard? Can they still lie?"

"It's a powerful drug, Sunny."

"But you said, *very hard*, you didn't say it was impossible. Can some people still lie, even with the drug?"

"It's unlikely."

"Is it a hundred percent unlikely?" I was getting very impatient.

"Nothing is a hundred percent unlikely." Billie responded kindly. "Why don't you take a rest, Sunny. You've been worn out with looking after Ben."

"He could have DIED, Billie!"

"He could have, but he didn't, and soon we'll find out if it was deliberate or indeed just an unfortunate mistake. Take a little rest. Here, I'll make this bed for you."

I didn't want to take a rest, I wanted to smash Jacqueline Roth's face. But Billie was a lovely woman, and she'd already set the bed for me, right next to Ben's bed. I lay down, fat tears streaming down my face. The magnitude of what might have happened crushed me like a megaton brick. I may have dozed off for a while, as I couldn't remember Billie leaving the room, and opened my eyes to find Violet lightly touching my arm.

"She was telling the truth, Sunny." Violet said softly.

"And you believe her?" I asked, accusingly.

"Yes, I do."

"What if she's resistant to the Truth Serum?"

"That is very unlikely." *Oh, here we go again...*

"But it's possible! It's still possible, isn't it?"

Violet smiled a faint little smile. "Rest up, Sunny, OK?"

She petted my hand and left me to simmer. I couldn't find any rest. My mind was racing. I felt I was about to explode. Without stopping to think it over, I hopped off the bed, and ran to the

Community Room. BAM! I smashed the doors open. Nope. Not there. Further down the corridors. BAM! I slammed through the doors into the kitchen-dining room with so much force, the doors bounced, whacking the walls on each side. All eyes were on me, but I couldn't give a damn. I found her, eating her dinner, all smiles and chit chat. My rage was beyond controlling. I pushed my way through until I was right on top of her.

"Sunny?" She stopped and stared at me; her eyes open wide. She wasn't smiling.

I bowed down a little so that my mouth was right over her ear. My voice was fierce and spiteful. "I heard you passed the test. I honestly don't know how you pulled that off, but you don't fool me. I warn you Roth, I am not the girl you remember from the farm anymore. I'm not afraid of you. You get anywhere near Ben again and I'll *kill* you. Do you understand me?" She nodded. I gave her another look, then turned around and returned to Ben.

23.

My feet buckled as I approached Ben's bed again. He was still sleeping peacefully, oblivious to the drama that only just took place, the tragedy that was averted. Tears began to stream down my face, as the enormity of his near loss dawned on me. Gently, I leaned my head on his chest, and cried. It was a good few minutes before I sensed the movement in the room. Hurriedly, I raised myself and wiped my tears, relieved to see it was only Phoenix. He was tenderly cleaning Leah's face, arms, and feet with a wet sponge, looking at me kindly. Phoenix was about ten years older than me. Rather handsome, softly spoken, nice young man. His gentle, somewhat introverted nature was rather at odds with the noisy company I had surrounded myself with, so our paths seldom crossed. In one of the early missions, before my time at the bunker, Phoenix was badly shot in the leg, and ever since then struggled with a slight limp. Since then, he rarely joined missions, but was a constant presence at the bunker, helping out where he could, supporting his close circle of friends and doing much of the outstanding cooking.

He silently put the sponge down, and approached me, as I was struggling to stop crying. Softly, he put his hand on my shoulder, and gave it a little stroke. His eyes were kind and thoughtful, his smile sympathetic. "Life here can get very hard sometimes," he said quietly. "Don't let her get to you, Sunny," he said. "Just, don't let her."

He lightly patted my back, gave me an encouraging look, then limped back over to Leah's bedside, where he picked up the sponge again. I watched him for a while. There was something rather calming in the peaceful, yet purposeful nature of the way he cared for her. My tears dried, my anger abated, but my mind was still busy. *Don't let her get to you, Sunny...* I couldn't help wondering, did he mean Jacqueline Roth... or Violet.

24.

Because of the sickness, the mission at the Fight Club had to be postponed, but now that most of us were restored to full health, it was due to go ahead within forty-eight hours. Ben was still recovering, which meant he was out. Leadership of Alpha One moved to Pearl.

I'm not sure what it was about that particular mission, but it truly scared me. Maybe it was the fact that this was a completely different industry to the one I knew so well from the inside. Maybe it was the monstrous, deformed fighters with their filed teeth that were terrifying. Maybe it was because Ben was not going to be there with me, and I felt like one of my arms would be missing.

As soon as people had recovered, we were back to preparing every night. There was comfort in knowing what you needed to do, step by step, but nothing could be taken for granted. Anything could still go wrong.

The day of the mission arrived. I was tossing and turning in my bed the whole night before, as was Pearl. In the early afternoon, just before it was time to hit the armoury, I went to seek out Ben. He was no longer in the Medical Ward, but in the usual room he shared with Nathan. He was reviewing the mission plans, which he would now observe from the Command Room. I was startled each time to see quite how much weight he'd lost while sick. His smile lit the room as I threw myself into his open arms.

"Hey…"

"Hey…"

"Watch out tonight, OK?"

I nodded, and suddenly tears pooled in my eyes.

"What's that for?" He whispered as his finger softly traced a tear that was rolling down my cheek.

"I'm going to miss you there with me…" I said quietly.

"I'm going to watch you all the way."

"I know."

"And you'll be amazing. Because you are."

I chuckled and looked into his eyes. His beautiful blue, blue, eyes, and I just dived into his lips, feeling my whole body going up in flames. I wanted to grab him, and feel him, and watch where that slim trail of hair led to, and *feel* it…

For a while he cooperated with me, and gave in to my craving, which was easily matched by his own. But then he suddenly pulled himself away, leaving me panting and bereft of his closeness. "What's wrong?"

"Absolutely nothing. Nothing is wrong."

"Don't you want to?" I asked, a little hurt.

"More than you can imagine," he smiled shyly. "But I'd rather… I'd rather we waited until *after* the mission."

"Why?"

He put his fingers through his ash blond hair. "I want you to have a reason to come back to me."

Huh?

"I want you to work extra hard at not getting yourself killed…"

"And… *this* would be the reason for me not to get killed?" I giggled.

"*Another* reason…" he smiled widely.

So, it had to wait.

*

Ben walked me to the armoury and from there to the prep room. For this mission, assimilating with the darkness was imperative, so we had to wear black balaclavas. I hated the feel of the balaclava on my face. It was itchy and made me sweat even more. We also smeared black paint around our eyes, where the skin was still bare, leaving only the whites of our eyes shining through. This too would change once the night vision goggles were on. Ben helped me put some black paint around my eyes. We chuckled as his paint-laden finger tickled me. "Look Up! Up!" He kept instructing me, but I couldn't help chuckling and closing my eyes, or looking at him, meaningfully.

"Do you want to hear something really strange?" he said suddenly, still amused.

"What is it?" my curiosity piqued.

"When I was still very sick and drugged, I had some weird dreams… like, really weird."

"Yeah? Like what?" *He has nothing on me with weird dreams.*

"I… it will be strange, I warn you!"

"Tell me!"

"I dreamed about… your mother…"

"What?" I did not expect that at all. "What do you mean?"

"I know, I never met her, but I've seen her through the Eye in the Sky… many times, and you do look a lot like her… I just knew it was her. I knew it instantly."

Now that was indeed strange. Why would Stella appear in Ben's dream?

"What… what happened… in your dream?" I needed to know.

"She just walked over to me, and she asked me to tell you that she won't be visiting you again."

My jaw dropped. "She sent me a message? In your dream?"

"Told you it was weird…" he smiled apologetically.

"And… that's it? That's all she said?"

"She also said something like, *nothing is as it seems.* Then she walked away. Disappeared."

We were both silent. I was amazed and deeply concerned. My mother used to visit me in dreams that bore meaning for my life. Often, they were omens for bad things that were about to happen. Why would she come to Ben? And why would she not come to me again? Was I about to get hurt in the mission? Or die? What were dreams anyway? Maybe it was all rubbish? Like those at the farm who used to believe I had some sixth sense, a gift to see danger coming. I never had. Maybe I was lucky once and earned that myth, but myth is all it was.

"I'm sorry. I didn't mean to make you sad…" Ben said, looking worried.

"It's OK. I'm glad you told me."

But it *did* make me sad, and more than a bit confused.

*

I kept pondering Ben's dream in the deep, dark, quiet solitude of the bus, on the way to our mission. I needed to know what it meant if anything at all. The more I thought about it, the less it made any sense. The less it made sense, the more I needed to understand it. Eventually, as the road stretched on and on, and our target neared, I decided to just let it go. If something ominous was about to happen, I would find out sooner or later.

25.

The underground fight club ring was not physically underground, but it was certainly in the middle of nowhere. In my mind, it defied logic that anyone would make it all the way out there, just so they could see men violently killing each other, while cheering them on. Clearly, I understood nothing about entertainment.

The building was a dull slab of bare grey concrete with large patches of old mould that had rotted it through. In the centre stood the large circular ring. It was impressively large, but terrifyingly threatening, once you realised what went on inside. All around, there were no windows, and only one central external entrance door for the punters, with their deep pockets and lust for blood. When pivoting to look at the building from the main entrance door, there were two external additions to each side. One, a large rectangle, the other a small square, so at odds in their solid sharp shapes to the ring that bounded them together. They seemed like two rotten cysts on an old bulbous nose. They too had no windows, only large, heavy bolted doors to access from the outside. I wondered if any fighter had ever tried to escape through that door. It was their only hope. Once they were in the ring, the only way out was to win with relatively minor injuries - or be carried out with the trash.

The smaller building was where the baits were held. We had no real way of knowing how many were in there, or under what conditions. The bank, where cash was kept, was about twenty meters north-east of the main entrance, in easy reach for punters who needed to cash large bills for further bets.

This psychotic entertainment centre was seeing action only once a week. It was difficult to draw people all the way out there more often, but the main reason had to be the cost of preparing a man to fight to the death. Each fight cost at least one fighter, if not two, depending on the severity of their injuries. There were several fights per night. It was not economical to run them more often.

The night was dark and chilly. The place seemed to be deserted, but for the sounds that proved the building was teeming with life inside it. Unlike the woolly farm that was so eerily quiet, the ring was alive with voices, but between the two, I preferred the silence. The noises that emanated from the ring were nothing I'd ever heard before. It was not the sort of noise I'd previously thought was humanly possible. They were sort of growls that were so deep and menacing, they rattled and vibrated through the ground and into the soles of our shoes. There was a moistness to them too, a sort of gurgle, as if these growls came out through some deep, tortured, bloodied cave. I could feel cold sweat prickling my back. Whoever made these sounds wasn't all human. Not anymore. I looked up at the circular ring top to make sure all four red eyes were already in position. If anything went wrong, these snipers were our only chance of getting out of there alive. The thought of being chewed up by one of those crazed fighters terrified me.

The one-minute empowering hug-circle of comradery and trust did nothing to alleviate our fears. It was almost a relief to be facing the door to the baits' cell, on the complete opposite side, away from the fighters. The heavy door was bolted and had an additional iron chain as a secondary lock. Pearl and Bill were hard at work with their heavy-duty bolt cutters, but the locks wouldn't budge. From the other side of the door, we could hear small moans and whimpers, soft and childlike, mixed with the rattling of chains. Imagine how deeply terrorised these boys were, how scared, how completely hopeless. From the little Violet had told us, these boys were kidnapped from their families. Ripped from their lives, thrown into this cell to be killed so viciously, how disorienting, and terrible it must have been for them. I was suddenly filled with real urgency to get in and take them out of there. But Pearl and Bill were struggling, and worse, they were tiring. At some point Pearl reached for her balaclava and angrily ripped it off her sweaty head, and soon enough, so did Bill. Those were all the cues I needed to promptly get rid of mine too. I wasn't sure what added value was in those hot, itchy masks. In no time, all the team's balaclavas were off.

"Simon, take my place," Pearl asked, as Simon quickly stepped in. Soon after, George was holding the bolt cutter instead of Bill. The clock was ticking. With every second, the chances of being found grew.

"Alpha Two to Alpha One, what's your status, over." Andy, leader of Alpha Two, was waiting by the bank, preparing to blow the thing to smithereens. He was becoming nervous.

"Alpha Two, some difficulty in getting the door to open, over." Pearl's voice was unsteady. She was clearly getting rattled too.

With a growing sense of urgency, George and Simon were now hacking at the locks. No more stealth mode.

"Fuck!" Pearl was agitated. "I think we'll have to blow up the door".

"Are you sure?" Simon wasn't ready to give up hacking. "If we blow it up, that's like putting a big, shiny, fluorescent red arrow pointing to our exact location, inviting any of the managers on location, and all of them freaking man-eating demons to get us."

Pearl was pacing nervously, biting her fingernails. This was her first mission as leader of Alpha One. The weight was heavy on her shoulders. "What do you think, Sunny?"

"Erm… with the noise we've been making in the past few minutes, there probably already *is* a big red shiny fluorescent arrow pointing to our location… Sorry, Si. If we blow the door, we can definitely get through, but we'll have a very short time to act. We'd need to get more people from Alpha Two to join and help us clear this cell of victims, and we'll need most red eyes on us."

Pearl put her hand on my shoulder and nodded. "Let's blow the darn thing open."

"Alpha One to Alpha Two, we're blowing up the door. We need two matches to join us ASAP."

"Roger that, Alpha One. Two matches on their way." Andy confirmed.

"Alpha One to Red One, we'll need full cover, over."

"Red One to Alpha One, we have you covered, over." Miley was the only one sounding excited.

And with that, all cogs of our mission were truly in motion.

"Josh, you're on," Pearl called. Joshua was tasked with preparing and attaching the explosives to the door. It had to be the exact amount to cause enough damage that would blow it open, but hopefully not harm anyone inside the room. He moved quickly, his hands sticking and tightening, peeling, and attaching. A real dance of calm and precision.

"Done," he announced as we all took several steps back and dropped to the ground.

"Fireworks display in three... two... one..." His hand clicked a small device, and the door blew open with a loud BANG, followed by a heavy thud that echoed for miles. From that moment, we had only a few short minutes to get in and free the children. There wasn't a second to lose.

We scampered onto our feet and ran as fast as we could towards the blown-up door. The cell was dark and damp and reeked of deep pungent smells of urine and fear. Inside the cell, cowered on the filthy floor, were twenty-five little children. It only then occurred to me how young they were. Each boy was individually chained to the wall by his arm. They were all in tatters, visibly trembling with overwhelming fear. Their dirty faces streaked with fresh marks of tears; they were whimpering softly. One boy was still holding a small toy in his hand. The scene was so grotesque it made me feel physically sick. With our weird-looking night vision goggles on, stepping through a smoking, blown up door, we probably did little to ease these boys' trauma. Each one of us darted towards one of the boys and used our bolt cutters to unchain them. Luckily, the chains that held them in place were easier to cut through than those locking the door. Still, it took some effort. I could feel my arms and shoulder blades stiffen as I exerted myself. It took several attempts, but I managed to cut the chain open. "Come with me. It's OK," I whispered and lifted the boy in my arms. There was no time to explain or gently wait for him to follow me, we had to move quickly. With him in my arms, I left the cell running. I could hear some of my friends running behind me. Some of the boys carried by the others were still whimpering, maybe even a little louder now. The bus was parked quite far, for safety reasons, and I could feel how the burden of carrying the boy was starting to slow me down. My breathing was quick and heavy. My throat was sore with the rapid inhaling of cold air. I sensed his little arms tighten their grip around my shoulders. "What's your name?" I asked him quietly.

Initially he didn't answer, but then, in a small voice he said "Alfie."

"Alfie. It's going to be OK." I managed to say, my voice bouncing in time with my steps.

I left Alfie by the bus, where Suli was guarding the boys already rescued. "See you soon, Alfie." I smiled and turned around, back to the cell, to rescue another.

The cell was emptier now, but still too many were left to rescue. Pairs of little eyes were watching me, begging. They all raised their chained arms towards me, pleading me to free them next. I picked up my bolt cutter and approached the nearest boy. My muscles were already tired from the first round, and everything seemed to take longer. I was working the bolt cutter with all my strength, when suddenly, the sound of a deep, terrifying growl nearby was unmistakable. The boys all jumped and started weeping. More activists had stormed into the cell, cutting chains loose and grabbing the boys out, to the bus. *This won't do. We won't have time to free them all.* I finally managed to cut the chain free of the boy I was liberating.

"What's your name?" I asked him. His teeth were knocking with the sheer force of his fear. "MMM.. Michael."

"Michael. Stand outside and wait for one of my friends to come back. OK? Stay outside, by the door. We'll save you. I'm going to free your other friends, OK?"

I showed Michael where to stand, and immediately went back in to unchain someone else. George and Simon returned, panting with the effort, immediately understanding what I was trying to do. Pearl joined us soon after, and we were all hacking stubborn chains, freeing more and more boys, leaving them outside and going back to unchain more. Finally, nearly all the children were free. Only one was left, the boy who held the toy in his hand.

The deep booming growl startled us all. It was loud and resonant this time, and close. Very close. "It's coming from behind the trap door!" George said in alarm. Terrible silence fell on the room. We could hear the rattling of chains from the other side, the menacing pacing, the sniffing.

"Pearl," I jumped in haste, "take the boys to the bus. I'll finish here and join you."

Pearl made the boys hold hands and run together as fast as they could. They were gone in seconds.

I picked up the bolt cutter and started working the chain with real urgency. Whatever is on the other side of the trap door, is not something I'd like to meet!

Simon came to my aid with his own bolt cutter, both of us exhausted from the cutting, the carrying, the running, the fear that was eating our energy away. We were nearly done when a terrifying shrill and the creaking of metal echoed into the cell. The boy screamed. The trap door… it was opening.

26.

The trap door was lifting, already we could see the ring revealed from the other side, stained with blood, reeking with the smell of death… There was a fighter there, we could only see his feet, but he was massive, and he was restless. The demon began lashing his way towards us, stopping short only due to the chain that was choking him. Again and again, he pounced. My fear was so real, I could taste it.

In one last hack of the bolt cutter, Simon cut the chain loose. I picked up the boy in my arms and together we all started running. I put all my energy reserves into sprinting as fast as I could, but the boy was heavier than Alfie, and suddenly he shrieked "My toy! My toy!" He wriggled in my arms so much; I nearly dropped him. "I lost it!"

"We can't stop!" I could hear the growls behind me soar, and what could only have been the breaking loose of a metal chain… and the quick, angry, ominous thuds of something big and terrible running behind us in the distance.

"But I lost it! It's from my mama!" He cried and wriggled.

His resistance forced me to slow down my pace. *What's wrong with this boy? We're being chased by a monster, and he's concerned about his toy?* Simon was already far up ahead. I didn't think Miley could reach me with her sniper gun anymore. I was by myself. Me and the boy.

The deep, wet, bloodied growls were almost upon us. The boy, all memories of his toy suddenly well and truly forgotten, hid his face in my neck and shrieked. The fighter was fast. I didn't think I had a chance. *It's better if I stop and draw my gun.* There was no time to think things through, if I didn't shoot, both me and the boy would be dead meat. I stopped in my tracks and put the screaming boy down. It couldn't have taken me more than a second to draw my gun, and another second to turn around and face my assailant. I gasped as he leapt at me; huge angry face, deep gaping jaws with large, filed-sharp teeth. It had once been a man, but I wasn't sure what it was any more. He was so strong, I dropped to the ground as if weightless, my gun flying out of my hand. At once he was on top of me, growling with such deep vibration, every cell in my body quivered. His eyes were dead. Drooling, his gaping chops were trying to close around my neck. I fought him back desperately, trying to push his face away, poke at his eyes, anything I could think of. But nothing could have prepared me for a battle one-on-one with something that so barely resembled a human being. I called on all my strength, all my fighting spirit that was left, and screaming from the pits of my soul, I pushed, hard, as hard as I could. Unbelievably, I managed to push the demon away as he was gnawing at air, trying to grab my face between his freakish teeth. He seemed momentarily stunned at the unexpected resistance, but before I had any time to collect myself, he leaped at me again, with renewed force. I screamed at the top of my lungs; sure, I was going to die. With diminishing strength, I prepared to push him off me again, my eyes shut tight. I didn't want to *see* myself being eaten alive, it was enough that I could feel my bones crushing, my flesh tearing. I could hear myself screaming. My screams were echoed by those of the boy, crouching terrified not far away. I could no longer help him. I could no longer help myself! I could smell the terrible stench of the fighter's open jaws. Soon I would be dead. *Ben! I'm so sorry… I'm so sorry…*

The fighter roared suddenly and reared up. His huge body contorted, as he drooled a mix of saliva and blood on my face. He reared up again, twisting from side to side, and staring down at me. His dead eyes piercing mine even through my goggles. Momentarily, he seemed a little surprised. His jaws still open, his body suddenly stiffened. Then he fell like a ton of bricks, crushing my arm, avoiding my face only by a fraction.

I was still screaming when Miley's face appeared over us. With some effort, she kicked the stiff body of the fighter off me. Only then I realised he was completely still. Miley reached for my arm and helped me up to my feet. I was sore and bruised all over, but I was intact. Nothing had been chewed off.

"Wow, he took four bullets before I finally managed to stop him. Sorry, Omega, I had to kill him. It was him or Sunny."

"Thank you, Miley." Ben's voice was heard through the comms. He sounded like he might be crying, and deeply exhausted.

"Hey kid, I believe this might be yours." Miley approached the boy, and handed him a small, blue train toy. He grabbed it from her without a word.

We walked to the bus, Miley supporting my aching body, the boy tagging along behind us. "Thank you." I smiled at her once we were finally on the bus. "You saved my life."

"Just doing my job." She smiled.

A loud blast shook the ground. The bank had been blown up. Mission accomplished.

27.

The only charity that was set up to deal with stolen bait boys was located a further three-hour drive north, at the foot of a beautiful mountain range. By the time we arrived, it was nearly dawn. A few women were waiting for us as the bus made its way through the gateway and into the wide yard.

The impressive mountains towered above us, their tips lightly dusted with snow. Tall, green trees covered the lower mountain slopes, like a festive lush skirt. I've never seen a place as beautiful as that.

One by one the boys were assisted off the bus by the women. The boy with the toy train still clutched in his hands, was asleep on the seat. "Come here little darling," said one of the women as she gently nestled him in her arms and carried him off. Last to get off the bus were the activists.

A short, plump woman with short and curly grey hair, very red cheeks, and a sparkle in her eyes, approached us. She wore blue corduroy overalls, and a name tag at her bosom reading 'Dorothy'.

"Welcome, Welcome." She said with a booming, cheerful voice. "I'm Dorothy, I manage The Lost Boys. Come in, come in, we have tea and biscuits waiting for you."

We followed her into one of the wooden buildings. A small entrance led us to a large hall. Scattered around were round tables, delightfully decorated with red and white tablecloths, surrounded with cushioned wooden chairs. Everything was made of wood, including the low, stooped ceiling. A fire was dancing in the fireplace, casting warmth and a sense of comfort in the room that smelled of smoked oak and of chocolate cake. A couple of round tables were brought as close together as possible and were heaped with tea pots and mugs, and large plates of biscuits and other types of mouth-watering bakery.

"Please, sit down. Help yourselves. Don't worry, it's all cruelty-free!"

I didn't realise how hungry I was until I took a bite from one of the date muffins. It melted in my mouth, sending warm fuzz into my aching body.

"You folks are incredibly brave," Dorothy said to us while pouring tea into our mugs. "We here absolutely admire you for taking such big risks, liberating the boys. You are heroes! Darn, if I were the leader of this country, you would all be knighted, or whatever it is we do with heroes."

"We're more likely to hang." Joshua smiled.

Dorothy nodded. "The times are changing. It won't be long before people will hail you for what you do. They will teach your names at schools. You'll see. I know it's true."

I sipped some of the tea, a strong but lovely brew with a peculiar flavour. "What do you do with all the boys?" I wondered.

Dorothy, sensing that all mugs were filled with tea and all stomachs were filled with food, finally sat down at the table with us.

"We try to find their families. It can take a long time. Some of them were stolen from far-away places. Some didn't even have families. Stolen from orphanages, or the streets. No one would claim them back. So, they stay here. We look after them like they were our own. But most of the boys go back to their families. It's those reunions, after all the terrible ordeals these boys suffered, that keep us going."

"So, how long do you think before these twenty-five will go home?" George wondered.

"Some families might be found within a week or two, others can take months. This will be their home for a while."

"Do they tell you, sometimes, about what happened to them?" I wondered. "As baits?"

"We provide medical and emotional help. I can tell you that some of the stories we hear would make your hair stand on end. Some boys wet their bed for years. I don't think they can ever go back to living just happy carefree lives. But... we try to ease their pain." She sighed deeply.

"Dorothy," Pearl broke the brief silence, "If they don't come here as rescues, with activists like us, how else do they get here?"

"Sometimes they are found wondering, sometimes a punter feels sorry for them and buys a bunch of them off, maybe trying to ease a nagging conscience after a night of gambling in the ring..." She grabbed a biscuit and looked at it for a while, maybe wondering if she should eat it or not, then putting it back down. "Baiting young boys is illegal, of course, but no matter how many times we file complaints with the police, nothing is done. The owners of those places are too powerful. They are untouchable..."

"They're not untouchable." I said quickly, "not anymore. Not with us. We'll bring them down."

Everyone around the table cheered.

"I believe you my dear, I do. But meanwhile, little boys are dying, and those people are getting richer."

The short morale-boost sank and drowned. She was right, things were happening, but they were happening too slowly for some.

Suddenly, something lit up in Dorothy's eyes again. With a renewed cheer in her voice, she announced, "oh, I nearly forgot, given it's now daytime and you can't drive back, we arranged some mattresses for you in the storage barn, where you can take a little rest. It smells a bit of apples in there, but it's nice and warm, and the mattresses are very comfortable."

As soon as she mentioned mattresses, I could suddenly feel deep exhaustion spreading through my body, loosening my muscles, weighing heavily on my bones, dragging my eyelids to close. I desperately needed some rest and judging by the look of everyone else around the table, so did they.

Dorothy made sure we ate until we simply couldn't eat any more and kept filling our tea mugs until the tea ran out. Finally, we were ready for our much-desired nap.

We stepped outside into the bright new day. The sun was already shining outside, the air was crisp and clean. There were boys running around the big yard, some were playing, some were carrying water jugs, some what seemed like baskets of laundry. Others were attending to the most beautiful and rare flower patch I'd ever seen. All were looking healthy and quite happy. One boy who was carrying a tray of what smelled like freshly baked loaves of bread, smiled, and waved at us. I waved back. I wondered what his story was. Who rescued him?

Dorothy led us through the yard towards the impressive barn on the other side. The large red building looked like it had only recently been painted. Inside it was airy, warm, and immaculately clean and tidy. It did smell of apples, but I found it quite appealing. Nine mattresses, fitted with pristine sheets, and matched with fluffy-looking covers, were awaiting us on the floor for the nine of us to lie down.

"Please, take a rest, you've earned it!"

We needed no further encouragement. One by one we dropped onto the warm, welcoming embrace of those mattresses like they were long-lost family members. I wanted to say something to Pearl, maybe it was "ooh, it's so nice," but I think I fell asleep before I even opened my mouth.

28.

I must have dreamed of demons chasing me, their teeth on my neck, their breath on my face, because my sleep was short and troubled. I woke abruptly, my back soaked in cold sweat, but surprisingly, all my aches and pains had disappeared. At first, I thought I must still be dreaming, but no, I was awake, and free of pain. *It must have been the tea,* I thought. My friends were all sleeping soundly on their mattresses, some snoring peacefully. I tried to give sleep another chance, but it only distanced itself further from me. Finally, I decided to get up and look outside. It was a rare, beautiful day. The sun was out and warm enough to put a smile on one's face, and the air seemed so fresh. The mountains, towering over the little sanctuary, were regal with their light crowns of white snow. There were sounds of laughter coming out of very cute looking, very neat wooden buildings. Giggles that were childish and bell-like, so innocent, as they always should have been.

I spotted the boy I'd seen before with the tray of fresh bread. Now he was raking the ground, piling up some fallen leaves. He noticed me and smiled, waving. I waved back and decided to approach him. He must have been about ten years old, quite slim; his dark hair was cut very short, and his teeth were as white as the snow on the mountains.

"Hi," I said to him as he kept raking absentmindedly, watching me come closer.

"Hi." He was smiling widely.

"What's your name?"

"Darius. What's yours?"

"Sunny."

"Oh, you're Sunny?"

I was surprised. He sounded like he knew about me. I must have looked puzzled, as he was quick to explain, "Dorothy told me about you. You're the one who escaped from Natures. The Dairy farm!"

Well, I guess I'm famous now. "Yes, that's me."

"Wow, you're very brave. I loved that story. My favourite!"

"Thank you, Darius." I said and smiled at him. There was something very laid back and innately happy about that boy. "So... what is your story?" I wondered.

"My story? Nah, it's not interesting. I'm like anyone else here."

"I bet there's something special about you."

"Nah. I was in an orphanage, and I was kidnapped. I was a bait, and then someone paid for me to be sent here so I wouldn't get eaten. That's all."

But that was awful. How come that was not a special story? What kind of world were we living in?

"I'm so sorry that this is your story, Darius."

"It's OK. I ended up here, which is better than the orphanage, so I'm fine." He said it like it was truly nothing special and kept raking the ground.

I watched him for a while, the warmth of the sun making me doze a little, when suddenly, from around the corner of one of those very cute looking, very neat buildings, something was walking toward us. Initially I thought I was back asleep and dreaming, but no. I was truly seeing it. Right there. Walking towards us. Slowly, confidently… What? How was it possible? I was so overwhelmed. My jaw must have dropped to the floor, and I may have even screamed, because Darius looked at me, a little horrified.

29.

"Sunny! There's no need to scream! Don't be afraid. It's only Bella!"

"Wha? Wha? How? I thought... I never..."

Darius giggled. "We thought so too. But one day, she just walked in here, walked through the gateway like she belonged here, proving to us that there are miracles, and that anything is possible!"

"But... they were all extinct! All of them!"

"Not all of them, obviously. As you can see, Bella exists."

Bella made her way towards us. She was large. Her beautiful, innocent, big eyes, complete with long, thick lashes, inspected me with interest. Her ears, large and poking to the side of her very large face were erect, and her two sharp horns were pointing upwards. She was absolutely stunning. White with black spots, one such spot was shaped like a love-heart on her wide forehead, and she had a big pink nose that was wet and shiny.

I could feel my heart beating fast, my breath rapid with awe and excitement. "I think I may have seen Bella before."

"Really? When?"

"It was quite a few months ago now. I saw her only briefly; I thought I imagined it."

"Now you know you haven't!" Darius was delighted. He dropped his rake to the ground and came to pet Bella on the side of her very muscly neck. She stretched it for him, clearly enjoying his attention.

"I wish Ben was here to see her!"

"Who's Ben?"

"My friend." I said and changed my mind, "my boyfriend."

Bella pushed her pink nose to my tummy. She was big, yet so gentle and playful somehow.

"She wants food." Darius said with delight.

The beast licked my face with her long, slightly rough tongue. I screeched with surprise.

"She likes you. She must know."

"She must know what?"

"That you're the same, you and her."

"What do you mean?"

Darius looked at me with wonder. "Don't you know?"

"Know what?"

"In olden days, cows like Bella used to be raised for dairy, like you."

I laughed. My laughter loud and hearty and rolling. Darius was a funny boy. But Darius's face had suddenly turned serious. He was offended. "It's true! Ask Dorothy! Ask anyone!"

Bella didn't seem to be very impressed with my incredulous laughter either and pushed her big pink nose into my sternum. I honestly thought he was joking. "Sorry, I didn't mean to offend you,"

I was quick to apologise. "It's just… she's a cow!"

"Yeah, she's a cow." Darius still wasn't consoled, "but in those olden days, people drank cow's milk!"

"But… that's just…" *choose your words carefully*, "silly."

"Yeah. People were silly, I 'spose. They drank cows' milk and not human's milk… I don't know why." He gave it some thought, then said, "d'ya know, they used to squeeze their tits!" The thought of humans squeezing cows' breasts for milk made him giggle, amused.

A dreadful memory of the night I stayed at the Jessop house, after escaping the farm, came to my mind. The way the rotten old man pushed his bony hand through my robe and squeezed my breast, like it was his to have. Like I was nobody, just a thing. Suddenly I sensed that there was a deep connection between Bella and me. Her ancestors once were treated as I was, like things, robbed of their milk, of their freedom, of their sense of self.

Bella's big, kind eyes were on me. I touched her large cheeks. Suddenly, I felt the urge to lean my forehead against hers. She sensed me. Our heads touched. We stayed there, connected like that, for a few moments. "I see you." I whispered. I just knew that she understood me. We were one.

30.

As night fell, we were back on the bus and on our way to the bunker. My thoughts kept drifting to Darius and Bella. I wasn't prepared to experience such a profoundly powerful connection with either of them, yet I did. More than anything I wanted to keep Darius in my life. I swore to keep in touch with him and come visit him at the sanctuary. As for Bella, by the time my friends woke up, she had already gone for a walk somewhere. She came and went as she pleased, and meeting more activists was apparently not on her to-do list. I watched her pace slowly into the distance, wishing for the opportunity to see her again one day. I didn't bother telling anyone else about my encounter with her. They wouldn't have believed me anyway. It was a moment I'd cherish forever, and it was mine alone.

Upon our arrival at the bunker, Ben was there, very obviously moved to see me with my face still intact.

His voice broke as he whispered "I thought you were going to die there... I watched as he attacked you... I thought... I thought I'd lost you!"

I smiled as I buried my head in his chest. "Miley saved me."

"She sure did." He sighed deeply. "But the way you fought that thing off you... man... remind me to *never* get on the wrong side of you!" He smiled, as his hand pushed my hair behind my ear, his lips close to mine, *very* close.

"Oi. Are you going to help us carry stuff from the bus, or are you going to just stand there and smooch while we're doing all the work?" Pearl had a point. I released myself from Ben's arms. "I should go and help."

He nodded but kept holding my hand. I laughed, "if I don't go help out, Pearl is going to smear my face with toothpaste tonight..."

"Then come and sleep with me."

Did he really just say that?

"I mean, in my room. Sleep in my room." He chuckled a little uncomfortably, but I understood him well enough the first time.

"I will... but probably not tonight." I laughed. "But you know... you owe me..."

"I know. I think I was rather stupid, to be honest." He pulled my hand and twirled me closer to him again. "I wish to repay my debt m'Lady."

"I'm sure we can work something out..." I giggled, as he kissed me softly.

"You still here, Ben?" Pearl was truly unimpressed. "Come and help out if you're that keen to stay."

Laughing, we hopped on the bus and helped clear out the gear. Things just had to wait a bit longer.

Two Years Since Joining DaSLiF

31.

It took a while for me to find my footing at the bunker again. My thoughts often wondered to The Lost Boys sanctuary, Darius, and Bella. Many times, I wished to visit them, but Violet was adamant with her refusal.

"It's too far away, Sunny."

"Ben and I can go and come back the next day."

"Out of the question. It's too far, the risks are too great."

"What's the worst that could happen to us?"

"With you, Sunny? Anything. Anything could happen. The answer is no."

It agitated me more than I cared to admit, being denied the liberty to go where I pleased, even though I accepted that danger seemed to follow me around somehow.

I found it hard to sleep at night. My dreams became consumed with gory arms, stretched through slits in trucks, dead eyes, maggot-infested heads, sharpened teeth, and all sorts of demons. True to her word, my mother didn't visit my dreams anymore.

Luckily, there was still the beach house visits, that allowed me to find my inner balance every now and then. In one such visit, I told Jonathan and Rose about Darius. I pleaded with them so relentlessly to go and visit him on my behalf, that eventually they did. Not surprisingly, Spirit and Darius hit it off like a house on fire. Both such innately happy, positive, and courageous kids. Jonathan and Rose were so impressed with him, they offered to adopt him. Plans started to take shape, forms were filled and sent back and forth, but the next time I came to the beach house, Darius wasn't there.

"He decided not to come," Spirit told me, with great disappointment. She liked him.

"How come?" I asked. It made no sense. Who would give up on the chance to live with a family like this one? *You did*, I reminded myself. *Well, sort of.*

"He didn't want to leave his friend behind," Rose said. "Such a sweet boy."

"What friend?" I was confused. Boys came and went from The Lost Boys.

"He's got an imaginary friend," Spirit whispered to me, "a beast named Bella."

My heart sank. Of course! Of course, Darius wouldn't want to leave her. She's a wonder. Spending time with her is like being touched by magic.

"She's not imaginary," I told Spirit later, once we were alone, picking up shells on the beach. "I've seen her."

"You've seen Bella? The beast?"

"She's a cow, and yes, I did."

"Swear it!"

"I swear."

"How is it possible?"

"I don't know. But it's just so."

"What was she like?"

I described Bella to her as accurately as I could. The heart-shaped spot on her forehead, her big, pink, wet nose, the way she moved, the way she licked me, the way her muscly neck felt to the touch.

Spirit's eyes lit up. Without warning she ran inside the house, shouting back at me "I've got to write to him! I need to ask him loads of questions! He was telling the truth!"

*

On our way back from the beach house, Ben and I were tasked with casually collecting intelligence on a sperm facility, about twenty-five kilometres out of our way. Dairy farms used this facility to buy sperm for impregnating their dairy slaves. It was forcefully taken from genetically modified males. We weren't sure if there were sperm slaves on site or whether the sperm arrived from elsewhere. It's that sort of information we needed to check.

"Don't go in there, just observe: Is it watched? How many people guard the place at any one time? The comings and the goings, the usual information we seek to begin with," Violet asked. "But Sunny, *don't* go in," she warned me again. *Why would I want to go in?*

I cherished the opportunity to spend time alone in the car with Ben. We still had no opportunity to be completely alone with each other since that afternoon in his room, before the Fight Club mission, and the longing was intense. Luckily, parking on the side of the road for some smooching, was the perfect cover for us.

Ben steered the car towards the roadside and parked at a strategic viewpoint. It was close enough for us to see all movement, and with the aid of our binoculars, we could observe faces, and even read lips, if we really tried. Ben leaned over to my side, to reach for the binoculars inside the glove compartment. As he did so, he stretched his body over mine as far as he could go. The warmth of his body radiating on mine, his chest on my chest, his lips immersed in my lips. *I wonder if we're actually going to collect any data, other than... on each other...* I thought to myself, smiling.

"What's amusing?" Ben wondered, his tongue playing hide and seek with my tongue.

"This. Us." I replied, my hand in his hair, my body tingling, completely alert.

"I know, it's ridiculous." He sighed and got back into his seat, binoculars at hand. "We should move into a room together."

I was taken aback by that comment. I knew that some couples were cohabiting in the bunker. Bill and Suli, Andy and Jessica, Simon, and Phoenix. But somehow, I never thought of it as an option for Ben and me.

"Is it something you'd like to do? To share a room with me?"

"Sunny, I'd like to share *everything* with you," he smiled, his eyes full of meaning. I could feel my cheeks warming. I don't know why I was suddenly embarrassed; I had blushed in front of him many times before, but still, I turned my head away from him, the sperm facility now in my sight. A few people were standing at the entrance. Something seemed odd. I thought I was imagining it. "Ben!" I snatched the binoculars and looked through them. I wasn't wrong. My eyes were not deceiving me. "Ben! Ben!" I gasped, and hurriedly handed the binoculars back to him. "Look!"

Ben put the binoculars to his eyes and his jaw dropped.

32.

"What the…?" Ben exclaimed. "I don't get it."

"Why would Violet send him here when she asked us? And why is he in there? Talking to these guards? What's the meaning of it?" I was confused.

Ben shook his head. "I don't get it."

"Is he undercover?" I wondered out loud.

"What's with the clothes he's wearing?" Ben was far from impressed.

"Well, if he's here, then maybe we're not supposed to be?" I suggested.

Ben was quite agitated. "She should've told us about this. Violet. She should've made us aware of that minor fact that he'd be here, undercover."

I couldn't agree more. It was ridiculous, and rather unprofessional.

"Let's go back," Ben suggested, his hands already on the wheel. "I need to have a few words with Violet."

We drove back in angry silence. It was absurd that we'd be assigned to a mission, as minor as it may be, without being given the whole picture. We parked the car at the undercover parking lot and made our way to the Control Room, where Violet spent most of her time.

"Back so soon?" Violet was surprised to see us. "And you didn't even go rogue and walk in?" she smiled.

I wasn't in the mood to reciprocate.

"Why didn't you tell us there was another mission going on in there?" Ben asked. He was clearly annoyed.

"What do you mean?"

"The undercover mission!"

"Ben, there is no undercover mission, what are you talking about?"

"If there's no undercover mission, then what was he doing there?"

"Who?"

"Nathan!"

33.

Violet was left speechless. I seldom saw her so obviously surprised. "You saw Nathan in there?"

"Yes!" Ben and I said in chorus.

"Peter, could you please go and see if Nathan is in the bunker? This is very strange. If he's here, please send him over."

In under five minutes Peter was back in the room, and… Nathan was right there behind him, still wearing his DaSLiF black t-shirt and black trainers. What was going on?

Ben was stunned, "You're here?"

"Sure mate, where else would I be?" Nathan was amused.

"We just saw you at the sperm facility!" Ben was not amused in the least.

"How could you have seen me at the sperm facility if I was here the whole time?" Now Nathan was losing his cool as well.

"Ben, Sunny," Violet interrupted, "tell us exactly what you saw."

We described the scene that we had witnessed. Someone who looked exactly like Nathan was standing at the entrance, talking to the guards. He was wearing grey pants and a striped shirt. "He was identical to you Nathan," Ben said, "even more so than Venus and Ren, if you could believe it! As if he was… a… a… "

"A twin?" Nathan asked.

"A clone."

We all turned our heads towards Peter. "A clone," he repeated. "We always knew the dairy industry was invested in sperm theft, but maybe the facility was also cloning foetuses."

"For what purpose?" I wondered.

"I don't know. Maybe to sell. It's all done for profit. Everything these facilities do is for profit, no matter how hideous."

"You told me your parents died in a car crash," Ben turned to Nathan, his tone accusing.

"They did!" Nathan was devastated. "I don't understand. Am I a clone? What does it mean?"

"I'm guessing you are," Peter said, his voice kind. "Maybe the facility clones foetuses that look just like you. How was it that you ended up with the people who raised you as parents, I don't know."

Nathan sat himself on the nearest chair, his head in his hands. "They never told me."

I patted his shoulder in sympathy.

"I'm sorry, mate." Ben whispered. "Sorry we broke it to you like this."

A melancholic atmosphere spread in the room. We'll never cease finding out more and more atrocities committed in the name of slave ownership…

"Nathan," Violet broke the silence. "We'll need to send you in there, for a *real* undercover mission. You know that don't you?"

Nathan nodded. He had already figured it out for himself.

"But first, let's get Jacqueline in here, and see what she can tell us about that place."

Yay.

*

Roth entered the room hesitantly. She noticed Ben and me and was obviously alerted.

"Thanks for coming, Jacqueline, please, take a seat. We just wanted to ask you about the sperm facility near the Winter Springs bridge. Do you know that one?"

Roth sat herself down, sending wary looks towards me as she did so. "I think I remember it, yes."

"What can you tell us about it?"

"Well…" Roth twiddled her thumbs nervously, "It's a well-known facility. They provide high-quality sperms for Natures and other farms. Obviously, there is great emphasis on providing females…" again she shot me a wary look, "f…for the… maternal milk… but they do manufacture males as well."

"Where do they get the sperm from?"

"From sperm slaves of course…" Roth smiled a grim smile. "You know, young, virile, post-pubescent males. They needle it out, then they modify it for improved quality."

"Do they keep sperm slaves on site?"

"Not to my knowledge, but… I can't say for sure. I haven't been there in quite a long time."

"Why do they manufacture males if the industry doesn't need them?"

"Well… for more sperm of course!" Roth chuckled nervously, then coughed it out. "Maybe also for selling to fight clubs, maybe to the meat industry. There's always some use for men…" She smiled and threw a quick look at Ben. I could've strangled her just for that. *Creep.*

"Jacqueline, do they do other things in there? Illegal things?"

"Like what?" Roth seemed unsure.

"Like cloning."

"Oh, I wouldn't rule it out," she answered casually.

"What for? Why have clones?"

"I'm not sure, but if I were them, I'd probably be cloning my best featured foetus, don't you think? The strongest, best looking, that sort of thing."

"And what would you do with those clones?" Violet kept pressing her.

"Sell them of course. There are always people who want to buy well-bred children. Especially if you can produce a shiny certificate to show how reputable these breeding-slash-cloning facilities are. Always a market for it. *Always.*"

34.

It was difficult to cheer Nathan up after that.

"They never told me. I always knew I looked a little bit different, but they told me my grandmother had slanted eyes... I believed them."

None of us knew what to say.

"OK," Violet said finally, "So here's what I think we need to do," and she drew us our next mission right there, off the cuff.

*

"I can't believe we're wearing this crap," Ben was tightening the belt on his khaki pants. I admit we did look rather ridiculous in our 'civilian' garb. I was in tight purple pants and a large, cropped green t-shirt. Ben wore a short-sleeved buttoned white shirt over his khaki pants, and Nathan was wearing dark blue trainers, a red jogging shirt and a baseball cap on his head, reversed, so that the front pointed backwards. "I mean, are we supposed to be disguised as a bunch of colour-blind idiots or something?"

We all had our guns hidden underneath our shirts, and small comms devices plugged into our ears. High above us, out of sight, was a smart drone. One of the ones Venus and Ren modified for us. We marched together, three oddly dressed individuals, directly towards the sperm facility, like there was nothing to it.

The guard at the booth by the entrance barrier stopped us, his look suspicious. "Can I help you, folks?"

"We're just here to ask a few questions about me." Nathan said casually. "I know I'm a clone and that I was manufactured here."

The guard looked us up and down under his bushy eyebrows, with unmistaken hostility. "D'you have papers?" he asked Nathan.

"No."

"How do you know you're from here, then?"

"My family told me."

The guard seemed to deliberate what to do with us. Finally, he said "go ahead."

We walked into the gated area, trying to appear innocent and nonconfrontational. The guard followed us with his eyes, speaking to his walkie-talkie. We were far enough not to be able to hear what he said, but the smart drone picked it up with ease, and through the comms system in our ears we received it as if we were standing right next to him.

"Another one in two days, what's going on with these defects?"

"Don't know Jonny. Stand by for quick termination."

"The girl too? She's hot. Check out her tits, man."

"You can have the girl, you horny old fuck."

I ground my teeth, trying with all my might not to run back, and put my foot in this man's jugular.

Innocently smiling, we walked into the facility like it was nothing but a candy shop.

"Howdy folks!" A balding man with thick glasses, his buttoned shirt too small to contain his bulging belly, his tie a little crooked on his chest, welcomed us in. "What can I do for you today?"

"My friend wants to know what the story is, with him being a clone and all," Ben explained, with extra politeness.

"What makes you think you're a clone?" the man asked, trying unsuccessfully to push his shirt into his pants.

"My family told me." Nathan said.

"I see." The man looked at us carefully. "Cloning is illegal, boy. We don't get ourselves involved in such activities here."

"Sir, I know I'm a clone and that I was manufactured here, so let's not play games." Nathan dropped the act.

The man seemed to contemplate his next move.

"Who did you say was your family, again?"

"I didn't."

"What's their names? I can look them up on our lists. Maybe they got sperm from us and mistakenly thought you were a cloned embryo?"

We all stared at him, silently.

The man combed the little hair he had, from one side of his head to the other, covering nothing. He was sweaty.

"Look, why don't you come to my office with your friends, and

I'll check our lists, eh?" He indicated with his hand that we should follow him. Holding the glass door to the inner hall open for us to go through, we walked in and waited for him to show the way. I could *feel* his eyes on me as I walked past him. He closed the door behind us and returned to his place at the head of our little convoy. The place was brightly lit. The walls, the floors, everything was white and smelled of disinfectant and lime.

The man showed us a little room to the side. It was small and almost bare. "Wait here, I'll be right back. There's water in that jug," he pointed to a little shelf where a jug of what looked like old, unclean water, was left. The door was closed behind him.

We refrained from talking as we suspected we could be being watched. We waited, pacing around the room, prepared for anything, our weapons ready for an easy draw. Meanwhile, the conversations were picked up by our invisible drone and transmitted into our ears.

"Hey Norman," it was the bald man with the glasses, "How come we get another defect coming snooping around? The second one in two days. I thought we took care of all that."

"We did, Boss." It was the voice who talked to the guard just before. "We covered all tracks."

"Well, clearly, not *all* tracks if two of these buggers come barging in here asking about where they come from."

"Well at least this one brought a good-looking pair of tits with him."

"Keep your dick in your pants, Norman, you idiot. I want to know how come they're still alive!"

"I don't know. We made sure all those families disappeared."

"Not good enough. We have a problem here."

"Don't worry Boss, we'll take care of it like we did with the one who came yesterday. He won't be asking anymore questions."

"Very well. Get your ass up here and finish the job."

"Roger that, Boss. Can I keep the girl?"

"No."

"I already promised her to Jonny, Boss."

"Fine. He can have a go with her, then you can have a go with her, then you kill her, now get your ass up here."

We looked at each other. It was showtime.

We took our positions strategically around the room and waited in still anticipation. Ben put his ear to the door, listening for the footsteps of the men approaching. Once they were close enough, he gave us the sign and we drew our guns.

"Sorry about waiting," the bald man with the glasses said calmly as he was walking into the room, his fake smile hanging onto his face for a split second before he realised the tables were turned. Behind him, and already storming into the room, were two men, the guard from the booth outside, Jonny, and another man, shorter and bearded, probably the one called Norman. Both had their guns drawn. Nathan punched the bold man in his face so hard, he smashed his nose, and the glasses flew off his face. Ben took Norman and I had the pleasure of finally denting my boot into Jonny's jugular. After overcoming the initial shock, both Norman and Jonny fought back. The bald man was subdued on the floor, tending to his bleeding nose, Nathan's gun pointed at his face. Ben and I wrestled with the other two. It took only a few manoeuvres for Ben to send Norman crashing to the floor. Jonny tried to punch my face, but I undercut him hard into his jaw, he groaned, bent forward, but kept aiming at me. I smacked the gun out of his hand. It hurled across the room. He wasn't happy, being outdone by a girl, still trying to grab my breasts with his hands, spitting, "come here you little cun…." My boot in his groin, planted hard between his legs, shut him up. He shrieked and dropped to the floor. We bound and gagged the two men, leaving the bald man to Nathan. There were still too many open questions he needed to answer for.

Outside the room, the sounds of softly running footsteps echoed through the corridor. The door to the little room opened. Romesh's smile was a sight for sore eyes. "You don't need any help here, I see." He chuckled. Behind him, fifteen activists were rushing through, deeper into the facility. He closed the door and joined the others.

Nathan made a show of loading his gun and pointing it directly at the bald man's forehead.

"I need you to tell me everything. Start talking!"

The man wasn't as brave as he seemed to be when there were two armed men behind him. Now he was shaking, his face and his shirt covered with the blood from his cracked nose.

"I… I… I don't know…" Nathan's hand smashed the man's face

again. I don't know why, but it made me jump. I didn't think it was necessary at that point. The man was practically pissing himself with fear. He'll talk.

"Ok… I'll tell you; I'll tell you everything. Please, don't shoot me, I have a family… children…"

"Talk!" Nathan wasn't playing.

"Yes… OK. It was, I don't know, maybe twenty years ago… there was this period of time when ginger was the hottest commodity." He looked at me, "not this sort of red-brown hair like yours, I'm talking real ginger, orange like. People couldn't get enough of it. It sent them crazy. Everyone wanted ginger children. Everyone. And they would pay. I mean they would *pay*. But true gingers are so rare, we couldn't find enough sperm slaves to produce that sort of liquid gold, if you know what I mean…"

"Keep going," Nathan urged.

"S…so.. we decided to just create one good embryo and clone it. It wasn't even illegal back then!" He looked at us for sympathy, "not like today… everything is changing." He wiped his face, then absentmindedly looked at his hand, suddenly realising he was smeared with blood. His eyes started rolling in his sockets.

"He's fainting!" Ben called in alarm.

Nathan reached for the dirty water jug and emptied it onto the man's face. The man splattered and coughed, dripping with stained bloody water.

"Keep talking!"

The man whimpered a bit, then continued. "Well, so… we decided to clone embryos for people who craved the ginge tinge. But something went wrong, the whole thing was botched."

"How do you mean?"

"Well look at yourself, dumbass, are you ginger?" the man asked in resentment, but this was only responded to with Nathan's hard smack of his face. The man groaned and spat on the floor. "They wanted ginger, we gave them Genghis Khan!" He laughed a short, spiteful laugh. "By the time you lot were born it was too late. Some families threw you to orphanages, other kept you. Your poor ma and pa probably loved you, eh? Miserable fucks."

Nathan smashed his hand into the man's face again, causing a new stream of blood to flow from his nose.

"Mate, slow down…" Ben said softly to Nathan. We were both uncomfortable with this modus-operandi. It was very unlike Nathan too.

"What did you do to them?" Nathan asked the man, ignoring Ben.

"Well, cloning became illegal, and these families were suing us for everything we had. They were becoming a… liability."

"WHAT DID YOU DO TO THEM?" Nathan shouted.

"Well, we had to remove the problem, didn't we? We had to finish them, that's what we did. Fried their asses, and YOU should have been WITH THEM you little piece of sh…"

Nathan's hand flew onto the man's face again. And then, again.

With the heel of his gun, he smashed the man's head, again and again. He was in a state of wild frenzy.

Ben jumped on Nathan and grabbed his hands, so that Nathan couldn't go on. "You're killing him mate, you're killing him."

Nathan was breathing hard, he was sprayed with blood and looking a little crazed. Suddenly he burst into a deep, agonising sob. Ben put his arm around Nathan. "It's OK man, it's over."

"They loved me!" Nathan cried. "They did! They did love me!"

"Of-course they did, mate. Who wouldn't love you, you knucklehead?"

Nathan smiled-cried. His body was shaking. I'd never seen him like that.

"Come on, I'll walk you to the car." Ben said softly, and together they walked out.

"Shiiiiiiiiiiit, what happened here?" Romesh was back in the room a few minutes later.

"Don't ask." I said, looking at the pool of blood and water everywhere. You couldn't even recognise the bald man's face anymore. "Is everything wired for some fireworks?" I asked.

"You betcha!"

We dragged the bloodied man and his two guards outside, as far as we could, away from the building. Five more employees that were found inside were already waiting out there, gagged and bound.

On our way to the cars, Romesh used the phone at the front

booth to call the Police and alert them that there were eight people in need of evacuation, and one who required immediate medical attention at the facility. Then, he pressed the little device in his hand and the building blew up.

35.

"I totally lost it in there, man." Nathan was in the back seat, holding his head in his hands, leaning against the door. "I just lost it."

We drove in silence. Nathan was still shaken, but no longer out of control.

"Hey, let's go to that food truck by the bridge crossing, and get some almond ice cream," Ben suggested. "It'll cheer you up."

"Sure."

We drove a little further, until we could see the food truck parked at the side of the road. A few benches were scattered around, where people could sit and enjoy their ice creams or hemp sausages. We were going to just grab them and go. As we parked, we saw that the side of the food truck was sprayed with a fresh graffiti, 'Fuck You Slave Lovers'.

Nathan remained in the car, while Ben and I queued to get the sweet treats.

"Been vandalized again, Joe?" the man ahead of us in the queue asked the food truck owner, pointing at the graffiti.

"Aye, second time this week," Joe, replied. "Some people just wouldn't give up the idea that sentient beings weren't food."

"They should try your food, it'll shut them up!" the man in the queue said.

Joe nodded and kept scooping out the ice cream.

Ben and I stood and waited our turn. As we stood there, we could clearly pick up a conversation being held on one of the nearest benches.

"Poor Joe. No wonder he was vandalized. It's those liberation activists. They make people so angry," said a teenaged girl with long bright yellow hair, streaked with pink stripes through it. "I just don't understand those activists. They're giving all of us a bad name, you know?"

Her friend, a rather pretty, darker girl with braces was nodding. "They're so extreme. Why do they have to be so extreme? Just don't eat those things and be happy."

"Uh-huh. They're not happy."

They were licking their ice cream with great attention. "I think, each to their own, you know what I'm saying? You do you. If you want to eat dairy, eat dairy! I respect your choice. I don't judge," said the yellow-pink girl.

Again, her friend was nodding. "No, I don't judge either. You do you."

Ben and I looked at each other, rolling our eyes. We got our three ice creams and made our way to the car, but I just had to… "Hey!" I called the two you-do-you girls. They looked at me without a shred of interest. "You know, I used to be a dairy slave. My best friend killed herself after she was raped. I saw my friends being raped in front of my eyes. My mother's children were all taken away from her, and all the boys were kept in jars. All of that, so that people could eat dairy. So, maybe you don't judge, but I do. I judge. The activists you slander, they are the only hope for people like me, so don't do you, because you suck!"

I left them there, staring at me, their mouths open.

*

Back in the bunker, we were immediately summoned to debrief Violet and Peter. Nathan, still covered in blood, fronted up immediately. "I messed up, Boss. I totally messed up."

Violet was not angered or upset. "What happened?"

Tears were rolling down Nathan's cheeks. "I lost control. I was so full of hate. I just went bonkers. I'm sorry. I could've killed him. If Ben hadn't stopped me, I could have." He wiped the tears off face, only to shed new ones. "Are you going to cast me out of DaSLiF?"

Violet looked at him carefully. "No."

Nathan's relief was absolute and endearing. He was crying now. "Thank you."

"I'm absolutely not going to cast you out, but I need you to go away for a while, to get your head screwed back to where it was before."

Nathan nodded.

"How long should I stay away?"

"Until you feel like you can come back without potentially smashing the faces of the opposition to a pulp. Take as long as you need," she said, smiling kindly. "Now, where should I send you? Is there anywhere where you can stay and relax? Look after yourself?"

Nathan gave it some thought. "I don't know if they'd take me, but... I wonder... Could I go to the beach house, to stay with Rose and Jonathan?" Nathan looked at me, "If you don't mind, Sunny... I love that place so much."

"Of course, I don't mind, silly. It's the best place to find peace. We'll come visit you." I gave Nathan a big friendly hug.

"I'm sure Rose and Jonathan would love to have you, but just to be sure I'll go and call my sister. Stay here."

We sat and waited while Peter offered us some water and snacks. Nathan seemed a little more cheered up. When Violet came back with an excited approval, Nathan went to his room to shower and pack a bag. Ben and I drove him to the beach house, where Spirit was elated with the new occupant, dancing around him, dragging him around the house, and already charting long, detailed plans of what they could do together each day.

"Spirit, Nathan is here to rest, not to be bothered..." I told her gently.

"It's OK, I don't mind," Nathan said with a smile. "I always wanted siblings. I think it can do me some good."

We had dinner together, and weird as it felt, we left Nathan behind and drove back to the bunker.

"You know..." Ben said as we parked underground, "it seems like my roommate is going to be away for a while..."

I looked at him, smiling. Suddenly, I could feel the little firebolts of energy and thrill shooting everywhere in my body. *Everywhere.* I could sense my breathing quicken, and my heart beating faster. Something inside me was gushing, asking, begging, *demanding*. Opportunity had finally knocked, and I just couldn't contain my desire a minute longer. I reached out my hand to Ben, and together we walked to his room.

As soon as the door was closed behind us, we were enthralled in a sensual dance of excitement and pleasure. At long last, everything we longed for was right there, in our easy reach. Finally, I followed the thin trail of dark hair that led from Ben's navel down, down... to wonderland.

Two and a Half Years Since Joining DaSLiF

36.

Nathan came back after two months at the beach house, with a renewed focus and heightened motivation. I can't say that I wasn't jealous. Even though Rose, Jonathan and Spirit were accepted by all as being my family, Nathan had probably spent more time with them than I did, as I had been whisked away to a life of activism so quickly after they took me in. His mentioning of Spirit as if he'd suddenly known her so well, annoyed me. She was *my* Spirit not his. I knew that no one could take my place as her big sister, but she was very taken with Nathan, there was no denying. He was an easy person to be taken with, especially now that he had managed to work though his rage issues.

Nathan's return saw a few shuffles in room cohabitation arrangements. Now that he was back, he reclaimed his old bed in the room he previously shared with Ben. It was clear that as our coupling status changed to 'serious', Ben and I would move into a room together. After four weeks of sleeping in Ben's single bed, we asked for permission to move in together, and a room for the two of us was arranged. Surprisingly, I discovered that sleeping next to Ben made me sleep better. Just the heat of him by my side, the weight of him on the bed, his presence alone, soothed my nightly dreams and reduced the number of nightmares I experienced.

I dreaded the moment of having to tell Pearl that I was permanently moving out of our shared room, but it could not have been avoided. As I entered our room to get my last few things, she seemed surprisingly cheered.

"So, you're moving into a room with Ben?" she asked, smiling.

"Yeah, sorry for ditching you like that, Pearl…"

"Oh, don't worry about it," she said sounding rather jovial. I hoped she'd be a bit sadder about losing me as a roommate…

"I love him… we're together. I mean, *together* together…"

"I know mate, don't worry about it. You should totally move in with him."

"OK…."

The door flew open and in walked Miley, carrying a large suitcase, and another small carry-on. She smiled at me, pushed the carry-on to stand by my old bed and threw her suitcase on top with some force. "Sorry, too much stuff. I'm such a hoarder…" she chuckled. "So… changing rooms, eh?" Radiating happiness, she skipped up to Pearl. "Hi gorgeous," she said with her warm, husky voice, and leaned into her, kissing her quite passionately on the lips. It took a while, but finally, the penny in my brain dropped. "You two?"

"Yes!" Miley threw herself on me for a hug and giggled. "And I hear you had something to do with this matchmaking idea too! Thanks babe." She kissed me on my cheek.

I couldn't stop smiling. "I'm really happy for you."

"And we are happy for you," Pearl said, as she winked at me, nodding to the door, "close the door behind you, eh?"

So, things had their way of working out. Even Nathan wasn't concerned about losing Ben as a roommate, claiming that being a solo occupant of a double room gave him the freedom to snore unreservedly.

For a while all was calm, loving, hormonal and harmonious. So naturally, it was time to mess it all up with a new mission.

37.

"Welcome, everyone!" Violet welcomed us to the board Room, presenting the sky map of our new destination. "Turner-Peterson Slaughterhouse, biggest death factory in the entire state, with the capacity of killing up to thirty thousand victims a day."

We all gasped. Thirty thousand victims were a number too difficult to comprehend.

"They don't slaughter quite as many anymore though," she was quick to add. "Those were the heydays of meat consumption. These industries have been in steep decline for a while now."

The place was enormous, built like a fortress, so that all the atrocities committed within its walls remained hidden.

Violet changed the image on the virtual screen, and the architectural floor plan of the slaughterhouse appeared. As she spoke, her purple marker indicated what was happening and where.

"As you can see, a heavy gate welcomes trucks into the slaughterhouse compound. Here," she pointed to a small building beside the gate, "is the security booth. The gate can only be opened either by the guard at the booth or when the truck drivers present a special electronic key that makes the gate slide sideways and open. They drive through here," She indicated the long, narrow driveway that led to the building itself. "Here, on the eastern side, is where the trucks reverse to unload the victims directly to a covered and secluded yard. This is where the victims wait, without food or water, for their time to die, sometimes just a couple of hours, sometimes a couple of days if there's a holiday." She tilted the view so we could have a glimpse of the yard and its link into the building. "To get to the kill floor from the yard, there's this path," she pointed towards a gloomy, narrow, dark, concreted path that was barred on all sides. "Here is where most struggles take place. In spite of what the industry tells consumers, victims absolutely do not want to die, and they know well enough where the path leads them. Workers use iron bars and electric prodders to force victims onto the path. Eventually the pain breaks them, and they go in. Once on the path, it is barred shut behind them, so that the only way is forward." She returned the view to the floor plan. "Once inside the killing floor, things move quickly. One by one they are stunned in their heads via electrocution, collapsing on the floor, but in no way dead. Sometimes still fully conscience, they are hung upside down, their throats slit open, and their body drained of blood, sometimes into buckets for the purpose of making black puddings, at other times just plainly onto the blood-drenched floor. It's not unheard-of to have victims still fully conscious at this stage." Again, everyone gasped. "Once drained, they are sliced, diced, and packaged for sale. Products for sale leave the slaughterhouse through the west side, here," she pointed with her purple marker, "loaded into commercial delivery trucks to go directly to supermarkets." She changed the image to the sky map again. "Our objective is to shut this place down, but here are the issues we have: This vile factory operates twenty-four seven. At any time we arrived, there could be trucks, there could be staff, and there will be victims. We'd have to evacuate staff, disable trucks, and rescue the victims before we blow the place up. But we simply don't have infinite capacity to transport hundreds of victims. We're limited to about two hundred and fifty, three hundred max. Another issue: see how massive the place is. We need a lot of explosives, and to place them strategically."

She put the purple marker down and sighed. "This will be one of our biggest missions so far, but it's not complicated, if we get the planning right. For starters, our drones can keep tally on victim numbers. We go in only once numbers are manageable and can be easily transported. In terms of explosives, we don't need to bring the entire building down, we just need to destroy the killing floor and its machinery. There wouldn't be too many trucks, as there simply isn't room for more than four double trailers at a time, so if we ensure the gate is sealed behind us, trucks wouldn't be able to go in and out, so all we'd have to deal with are the trucks already on location." She paused, took a sip of water, and looked at me. "The advantageous point is, we have information from Jacqueline Roth. Transports from Natures farms across the state, only arrive on Thursday nights. So, Thursday nights are Natures victims only. That means better controlled numbers, and trucks that can be easily disabled due to their unique immobilising system. It also means victims will be mostly or all women, some could be pregnant."

"They send pregnant women to slaughter?" Miley was stunned.

"They do, if their milk production isn't profitable enough to keep anymore," Violet explained. "These women were impregnated again and again since they were about fifteen. At some point their body just gives in. Some women get terrible cases of uterine prolapse, that's basically when their entire pelvic organs collapse. Others have such bad mastitis; their breastmilk is nothing but pus and blood…" She sighed, looking at me again, "most slave women in the dairy industry don't live to see thirty-five."

She kept looking at me, then moved her gaze on to Pearl. "Having our mission on a Thursday, might also mean, victims we actually know."

Pearl and I swapped horrified looks.

For the first time since I joined DaSLiF, when the floor was opened for people to contribute their thoughts and proposals, I had nothing to give, and my friends were surprisingly all silent for a while too. It was Pearl who eventually broke the silence, "So, when we go inside to put the explosives, there will be bodies hanging there, blood dripping, cut to pieces and all that?"

"It is the most likely scenario," Violet confirmed.

"And those could be women we grew up with, Sunny and me?"

"Yes."

"Could be my mother?"

"Yes, Pearl. Theoretically speaking. I understand if you decide not to participate in this one."

Pearl swallowed hard but didn't leave the room. I could tell that Miley was holding her hand under the table, the way that Ben was holding mine.

Slowly, people began to come up with suggestions about how to approach this mission. There were plenty of options, plenty of risks, plenty of things to take into consideration, plenty of ways to crumble that cookie. Hours passed and still no concrete plan was agreed. The main point of disagreement was whether we needed to sneak-and-surprise or storm the place with guns blazing. In the end, after so much deliberation, and when we were all fairly agitated and restless, a middle ground was reached: The first team would sneak in, for the purpose of disarming and taking control of the security booth, which also controls communication with emergency services. Once that part was done, our buses would storm inside via the main gate, which would be closed behind us. Trucks already inside would not be allowed to leave. Once inside, we would be divided into four teams: the first team in charge of disarming and evacuating workers, two teams in charge of liberating victims, and the fourth in charge of wiring the place with explosives.

Once again, I was assigned to Alpha One. Nathan was to lead, and with us were Ben, Pearl, Romesh, George, Bill, and a couple of new activists who joined only several months prior, Suzy and Alice.

It was past midnight when we finally dragged ourselves out of the Board Room. We had three weeks to prepare and get ready, starting the very next day.

38.

Imagine the extent of my surprise when out of the bunker, during our first training session, came no other than Jacqueline Roth. "What is *she* doing here?" I whispered to Ben.

"No idea."

The three teams in charge of evacuations were all there, with the buses parked nearby. We were practicing victim evacuation into the buses, anticipating mayhem and disorder, especially in large numbers. Given that Alpha One were not in charge of liberating victims, but workers, we were role playing victims for that particular session.

"Can we help you, Jacqueline?" Nathan asked, as Roth approached us.

"Oh, don't mind me, I'm just here to observe," she said with a smile. "I may get more involved in the next mission, so I need to learn."

I couldn't believe Violet would ever allow Roth to participate in a mission. Her being there with us felt completely out of line.

Nathan, Ben, Pearl, and I all looked at each other, shrugging our shoulders, but it seemed only I was truly disturbed by this new situation.

"You should stand over there, Jacqueline," Nathan indicated a position further away from the group, "we don't want you to get hurt."

"What if I have a question? Shouldn't I be standing a little closer to you all?"

"How about you make a note of all your questions, and I'll do my best to address them later, OK?" Nathan responded with commendable calm and respect.

Roth nodded compliantly and took a few paces towards the point where Nathan asked her to wait, but not all the way back. I felt the blood steaming in my head. Couldn't this woman just *disappear*?

We simulated various situations, mass panic, injuries, stampedes, as many as we could imagine. It was impossible to prepare for absolutely anything, however having the confidence to deal with impromptu situations was partly why we attempted to cover as many as possible.

We spent hours running, struggling, being picked up, carried, loaded onto the bus, downloaded off the bus, calmed, soothed, and ordered around. My body was bruised from all the times someone picked me up, dragged me, carried, or pushed me on. Every now and again I angled a look towards the spot where Roth was standing. She was still there, watching us. The night was growing colder, and I felt a growing need to go to the toilet, but the next toilet break was still an hour away.

"Are you OK?" Ben asked as I was starting to show signs of impatience.

"Need toilet."

"Can you hold?"

"For now."

But soon enough I realised that I couldn't delay it any longer. Grating my teeth was not helping, I had to go.

"I need a toilet break," I told Nathan. "Urgent."

"OK. Can you go somewhere outside here? Maybe behind the buses?"

"Sure."

It was dark enough that I could do my business ten meters away and no one would have seen a thing, but to be more discreet, I walked further towards where the buses were parked. Looking around me, just in case, the coast was clear. Release was sweet and blissful. The heat of my urine in the cold night crated a little mist, which made me smile. Concentrating on the sound it made, pooling on the dry ground, it suddenly occurred to me that there were other sounds nearby. Not the activists, but something else completely. The sounds intensified. Someone was there.

"Hello?" I called into the darkness. "Don't come here, I'm pissing!"

There was an odd sense of movement. Someone was running. I quickly stood up and pulled up my pants. "Who's there?"

It was too dark. I could only hear the sound of hurried footsteps on the ground getting closer and closer. And there was something else, but I wasn't sure what.

I looked around, trying to pre-empt the obvious surprise, when

WHACK! someone smashed hard into me, throwing me on the floor. My assailant fell on top of me, grabbed me by my shirt and tossed me further away, rolling me over to the side. What was going on? My back hurt from hitting the ground and my mouth was full of dirt. I spat it out, but my assailant was still holding on to me, trying to roll me again. I quickly regained my senses and pushed my attacker off me. By the build and body mass I could tell it was a woman. I grabbed and tossed her on the ground, rolling over her, pinning her down between my legs, one hand holding her right shoulder in place, the other ready to punch, hard.

"Who are you? What do you want?"

"It's me! It's me! Don't hurt me!"

WHAT THE ACTUAL... "Roth? What the heck?"

"Don't hurt me!" she shouted quickly, "Look!"

Where I was only a moment ago crouched in peace, happily urinating, a bus was rolling backwards, picking up speed. "I tried to save you... from the bus... I could see it was rolling... I didn't know how to stop it.... "

More footsteps could be heard now, mayhem broke. Nathan was shouting as he jumped into the rolling bus, Ben was calling my name with some hysteria.

"I'm here!"

He came running to me, Roth was still pinned down between my legs.

"What's going on?" he asked, confused.

"I… well, I was… the bus… and she… she saved me…" the way I said it conveyed how incredulous this was to me. "Roth saved me." I removed myself off her and helped her up to her feet. Roth wiped her clothes with her hands. I was still confused. How was it even possible? According to everything I knew about her, she was supposed to push me under the bus, not away from it.

"What happened, Jacqueline?" Ben asked.

"I saw the bus was rolling backwards, I tried to call you, but you were all preoccupied with your activity, no one was paying any attention or looking at the bus. So, I ran to get Sunny out of the way."

Nathan drove the bus back into place, switched the engine off and joined us. "The hand break was down," he said, confused.

"How come the hand break was down?" Ben wondered; he was clearly very upset.

"I don't know, maybe it was pushed by mistake during one of the simulations?"

Ben was still unsatisfied with that. "What did you see, Jacqueline?"

"I told you; I saw the bus starting to roll backwards, and I knew Sunny was there."

"Who checked the bus before we started?" Ben asked.

"I did. It was fine when I checked it." Nathan was getting annoyed.

I stood there numb with the realisation that Roth, my biggest nemesis, just saved my life. What if everything I thought about her was wrong? What if she really *was* turned, and all was forgotten between us? I didn't know how to process all that new information. My head was spinning.

"I'm calling this session off," Ben said angrily, and took my hand.

I wasn't sure what to say, but one thing had to be said. "Thank you, Roth."

"It's OK."

*

It was very late, my eyes were nearly shut, my head was leaned against Ben's chest, my arm sprawled across his abs, his arm around my body, his fingers softly tickling my back, playing with my hair. He was wide awake, his eyes staring at the ceiling.

"What is it, Ben?" I asked, my voice sleepy.

"What if *she* did it?" he asked.

"What if she did what?"

"What if she pushed down the hand break, then pretended to save your life?"

That line of thinking, trying to find fault with everything Roth did, was usually mine. It was odd to suddenly share it with someone else. "Why would she do that? What could she possibly gain from it?"

"Your trust."

"But she was with you guys the whole time, quite far from the buses too."

"No one was watching her the whole time. She could have sneaked out of there."

"So, you think she set the whole thing up?"

"Maybe she just acted on a whim. I don't know. I don't trust her."

Now? Now you suddenly don't trust her? After I've been on her case for two and a half years?

"Do you think she had enough time to both trigger the rolling of the bus *and* save me?"

"I don't know. Maybe. I just can't stop thinking about it."

"I'm so confused, Ben. Maybe you're right. I'm still very wary of her. Something about her isn't right. I agree with you, I still think she's not to be trusted. But I don't know about this one. She seemed honest... I don't know..." I raised my head and turned his face to me, "but I love that you're completely on my side," I smiled and kissed him.

"I'm always on your side, Sunny."

39.

In essence, nothing had changed. I still tried to avoid Roth in any way possible and couldn't deny that I still felt deep distrust toward her. Ben's suspicion that she orchestrated the whole 'bus rescue' thing, kept playing on my mind. It was possible. Still, since the bus incident, I attempted – with varied degrees of success - to be less hostile.

Roth still came out of the bunker to observe our practice sessions each night, bet kept her distance, and I no longer took non-scheduled toilet breaks.

Three weeks later, on a Thursday, we were ready to strike.

Turner-Peterson Slaughterhouse, or as they preferred to call themselves "Processing Factory", was a two-hour drive north from the bunker. In four buses, we made our way out as night fell, each bus twenty minutes apart. Ahead of us, a car with five activists, led by Joshua, left on their mission to take over the security booth. The buses congregated on a side road, less than ten minutes away from Turner-Peterson's front gate, where we waited to hear Joshua giving us the All Clear.

Waiting in the dark for a signal, not knowing what was happening, could be stressful enough when the signal arrives in a few short moments, but waiting over half an hour was excruciatingly testing. *Everything is fine*, I was telling myself, *we sent the best team for the job.* Instead of thinking of what might have been going wrong, I kept running the plan over and over in my head. No one in the bus spoke, but you could sense the tension.

Finally, after thirty-five long minutes of waiting, Joshua's voice came through the comms. "This is Alpha Five. We have the booth under control."

Nathan switched the engine on, and we were off.

Turner-Peterson "Processing Factory" was off the main road and out of public sight. No one wanted to see victims going in alive and coming out as wrapped packages. Having it all done *somewhere else*, negated one's need to think about the ethical challenges of having slabs of flesh for dinner.

The bus was rolling fast. Activists were standing outside the booth, controlling all movement. The gate was open for us to drive straight in. We made our way up the narrow road leading to the main building. The place was enormous. Two double trailers were parked on the eastern side, likely to have freshly unloaded their victims. Nathan steered the bus around them and kept going. Through the windows, we saw the yard where victims were waiting their turn to be slaughtered. There were at least one hundred women out there. I felt my heart beating fast. What if I knew them? The women I grew up with? Knowing that this could have been my own destiny, to end up there, was hard to accept.

Nathan parked the bus and we all hopped out. First, we had to disable the trucks. Natures trucks were all very modern, with special immobilising devices, apparently due to heightened numbers of them being overtaken by activists all over the country. We ran towards the vehicles, making our way around the outer rim of the victims' waiting yard. The trucks were empty. Their drivers probably inside, having a cup of tea, or a laugh with the staff. After all, they were just 'doing their job' as Larry, the driver Ben and I intercepted months ago, told us. Bill and George immobilised the trucks and destroyed the devices, rendering both undrivable. Quickly, we ran back towards the building, but the rise of deafening screams made us stop in our tracks. Two employees were coming out to start prodding new victims inside the kill floor. Both were holding electric prodders. They also had stun guns. The victims' screams of terror curdled my blood. Pearl and I looked at each other. Without hesitation, we jumped the employees from behind. It was an easy job, really. These men weren't fighters or guards, there was no requirement for them to be combat savvy. In thirty seconds, we had them tied up and gagged. We now had two electric prodders and two stun guns added to our arsenal.

Circling the yard, back towards the staff door, I made every effort not to look at the women who assembled there in fear. As I reached the door to go inside, I thought I heard someone whisper, "Sunny?" it could have been just my imagination. I didn't recognise the voice. Maybe it was the wind. I hesitated for a split second and looked out at the yard. One of the women broke off the main huddle. Was it her? The one who called me? It was dark. She was just a rugged-up woman. I couldn't tell who she was, if she even called me. Alpha Two and Alpha Three were already there, shepherding the women into our buses. It was more plausible one of our activists was the one calling. I walked in, closing the door behind me, facing the full effect of the killing floor.

Don't look. Don't look. Don't look. Just spot the workers, disarm, control, evacuate. Disarm, control, evacuate. Simple. But it wasn't simple. Alpha

Four were already on site. They stopped the killing line. Everything was still. Bodies who were only seconds ago a living person were now hanging limply upside down, naked. Blood was streaming all over the floor. It was slippery, and humid. The stench of charred flesh, fresh urine and faeces knocked the wind out of me. Fear made victims defecate just as they were being killed. Some victims were still moving their limbs, still not dead, gasping for air while choking on their own blood. I felt my head going dizzy. My stomach churned.

"Sunny!" Ben shook my shoulder. "Are you OK?"

"Yes. I'm fine." Tears stung my eyes. *Get a grip, Sunny. We have work to do.* Alpha Four were already wiring the columns around the kill floor, attaching explosives to the gory slaughter machines. I ran further in, trying not to slip on the blood and urine. A couple of workers were attempting to hide behind the soda machine. *They have a soda machine on the kill floor!* Bill and I grabbed them. They did not struggle. It was almost as if they *wanted* to be taken away from there. I led them both out towards the staff evacuation place, away from the building, leaving Bill to grab another employee. They came willingly and without any struggle. While outside, I turned my head towards the yard. The buses were being filled with victims. The ragged-up woman wasn't there. Maybe I imagined it. Alpha Two were already leaving the place, their bus crowded with liberated victims. I ran back in, passing Ben with a couple of employees on their way out. "Check the toilets," he said. I ran up the stairs. There was a large room with a glass window, overseeing the kill floor. Probably the main office. Inside, workers were being tied together and gagged. No one fought back. I kept running through the corridor. Barging through the toilet doors, I found two staff women cowered on the floor by the basin. I don't know why, but it felt odd to see women employees in a place like that, wearing nice clothes, high heels, and makeup. I'm not sure why I expected them to have more empathy. I should have known, from my own experience, that a person's gender meant nothing, but still, it felt odd. "Please don't kill us!" they whimpered, their hands up in the air. I tied them up and stuck a tape on their heavily lipstick-adorned mouths. How bizarre were these women, I thought, begging for their lives. Clearly, their lives were precious to them. But life was precious to each and every one of their victims too. I left them there while checking the men's toilets as well. Ben was back upstairs now, with Bill and Pearl, kicking doors, checking behind bookshelves and under tables. There was no one else. I grabbed the two women and walked them outside. Alpha Three were already gone as well. The victims' yard was empty. Josh was waiting for us on our bus, there were victims loaded in it as well. Bill stayed behind to guard the evacuated workers. He'd be joining the fourth bus with Alpha Four after the explosives were all set to trigger. We hopped on the bus and started driving away. Two minutes later the earth shook with the sound of explosion. Soon after, the rest of the teams were out of there. Mission accomplished. For such a gory mission, in such a large and intimidating place, the mission was the fastest and smoothest one I'd experienced so far. It was strange, how compliant the workers were. There was no struggle at all. Almost as if they wanted that place to burn.

40.

Back at the bunker, the parking lot was crammed with people. The Medical Ward was too small to contain everyone, so only the very sick, the pregnant and the injured were taken in. Blankets were spread on the floor, with as many pillows and cushions as could be found, scattered around for more comfort. A table was quickly set up by the wall, with a generous selection of fruit juices and cupcakes. In addition, we passed through the crowd with water jugs and glasses, offering fresh, cold water to all those who were too tired to get to the table. I looked carefully at all the faces, but I couldn't recognise any of the women there. I saw Pearl walking the floor as well, offering water, looking at faces. She was hoping her mother would be there. We met back at the table, refilling our jugs. "Recognise anyone?" She asked.

"No, not one. I don't think it was our farm."

"No." she was deeply disappointed.

"I'm sorry, Pearl. I know how you wanted your mother to be here."

She nodded. I could see her eyes were glistening with the hint of tears. "Well, maybe it's a good sign though. Maybe it means she's still alive, eh?" I smiled a faint smile, nodding lightly. She was silent for a while. "You know," she said, looking at me, "I wasn't very close to my mother at the farm. It was almost like she gave up on me. I think most girls had that. We were kind of abandoned by them, you know?" I nodded. "Except for Stella. She was still so involved in your life. We were all jealous. You still had your mother to care about you."

I was taken by surprise. I didn't feel like my mother did a particularly good job with me, more so than the other women. "I felt abandoned too. Especially after Hope died."

"Really?" Pearl was amazed. "Huh." She sank into her thoughts, dropping a couple of ice cubes into the water jug. "I still wish we could save them."

"Of course. We all do."

We circled the room a few more times, offering water. Slowly, the women were settling for a night sleep, or at least an attempted rest. It was incredible, seeing the sea of living humans on the floor, all could have been dead by then. One hundred and forty-six women were saved. We should all be so proud. Starting tomorrow, these women will be sent to sanctuaries to live out their lives in peace. There could be no better reward for our efforts.

I made my way towards the residential quarters, passing some women queueing at the public toilet on my way. I smiled. Women always queued at the toilets, but tonight the line was so much longer than usual.

At the point where the corridor started to widen, Ben caught up with me. He had spent the last few hours assisting at the Medical Ward. He put his arms around me, kissing me long and soft. Finally, he whispered, "you need to come to the Medical Ward with me, Sunny."

"I was just about to go to bed," I said.

"I know, I'm knackered too, but you need to come with me, first."

"Why? What's the matter?"

"There's someone there asking about you."

41.

All the beds at the Medical Ward were occupied. Ben led me through the room, to one of the beds furthest in. A woman was lying there. She was so thin, almost skeletal. Her eyes were sunken, her skin pale and flaky. I couldn't recognise her. She opened her eyes in what seemed like some great effort. They were the colour of dull blue. Something in her face started to fit with an image of a woman I once knew. But it was nothing but a faded echo.

"Sunny?" she called my name, her voice croaky and hoarse.

I took a few steps closer, staring at her face, trying to put the puzzle together in my head. She couldn't possibly be… "Freckles?"

"You remember."

Freckles was one of my mother's closest friends at the farm. Aside from Stella, she was the second most formidable woman I knew, growing up. Bossy and confident, I used to look up to her. I used to be slightly afraid of her, to be quite honest. The woman on the bed wasn't the Freckles I remembered. "What happened to you, Freckles?"

"Cancer," she said quietly.

I made the last step towards the bed and took her skeletal hand in mine.

"Can you believe, they still sent me to the slaughterhouse?" she asked, coughing a little. "There's nothing left in my body to consume, still they sent me. Like trash. Could've just left me to die in peace, in my bed, but no."

She observed me with great care, her weak hand tightening in mine. "I'm sorry about what they did to Stella."

I nodded, feeling the tickle of tears in my eyes.

"Poor Stella. It's a travesty, I tell you. A travesty!" she burst into a chain of rusty coughs, that left her weakened. "But you are a joy to look at, Sunny. Everyone would have been so proud of you."

"How is Antim?" I asked, bracing for bad news.

"She's just the most beautiful girl, Sunny. She looks so much like you."

I smiled, the tears finally breaking off and rolling down my cheeks.

"She's also a pain in the ass like you..." Freckles smiled. "Independent and determined, can't teach her anything..."

I laughed. Antim was just a wee toddler when I left. I missed her.

"The place hasn't changed much since you ran away. Still a tit slave stinkhole. All your friends have been through two birthing cycles by now." Her tone was very matter of fact, but I felt my tongue stick to my mouth. "Off to The Shed every day, get their milk pumped out. Some life! I wish I had the guts to touch the fence like your friend, Rosy Cheeks. Way more dignified"

I gasped for some air. How was that dignified? I can still recall the smell of Rosichi's burned flesh, her pretty body plastered lifeless on a tree, after being thrown by the sheer force of the electric shock.

"One of your friends, Flower, remember her? She died at childbirth. Was her second one. The boy died too, of course."

Suddenly, I couldn't take any more of that grim report that Freckles was giving me. The way she told it, so dry, so lacking emotion. What happened to her?

I gently took my hand away. "I should get some sleep now, and so should you," I smiled.

She nodded. "You were always the strongest one," she said, her eyes closing.

I kissed her gently on the forehead and watched her slowly fall into sleep. Leaning onto Ben's arm, tears kept rolling down my face, as memories of my mother, of Antim and my friends kept flashing in my mind. Knowing that their grim destiny would have been mine to share, if I hadn't escaped.

"Ben, let's stop at the Command Room first, please." I asked him, as we made our way to our room.

"Why? It's late. Command is already shut down for the night."

"I need to talk to Violet."

"She's probably not there anymore. Can't it wait 'till morning?"

I nodded. Yes, it could.

*

The next morning, two things happened:

I saw Violet and demanded that our next mission would be storming in and taking down Natures Farm. *My* Natures Farm.

A couple of hours later, Freckles died peacefully in her sleep.

Two Years and Eight Months Since Joining DaSLiF

42.

"I want you all to welcome two brilliant activists who are joining us from one of the southern cells to help with planning and executing our next mission," Violet announced to a full Community Room. There was excitement in the air. "Their cell has managed to shut down two Natures Farms in their region. So, you see, it can be done. And given that our next mission is storming the Organic Natures Farm that was kind enough to give us Pearl and Sunny..." Cheers and whistles erupted around the room, "...we thought it would be helpful and rewarding to ask them to join us for a few months..." Everyone clapped. I looked around the room, keen to see what Jacqueline Roth's reaction was. I spotted her standing close to the door. She was clapping with everyone else, looking pretty pleased. "I'm very happy to introduce to you Dominique and Carl."

The two southern activists stood up from where they were sitting and waved to the room.

"Maybe you could tell us something about your DaSLiF cell?" Violet suggested. The two activists nodded.

"Hello everyone, thank you for the warm welcome," Dominique smiled to the room. "It's a pleasure being here. We were always very keen to visit the original, first DaSLiF cell. You folks are legends in the south..." Her words were received with cheers and whistles of pride and satisfaction. "I don't know if you're aware, but Peter used to be one of ours before he relocated." People cheered, and Peter waved to the room, smiling behind his bushy beard. "Our cell, where

Carl and I come from, is smaller than yours, but down south there are at least three others like ours, so all in all, there's quite a lot of strength in the south. We do a lot of slaughterhouses shutdowns, and we recently had two very successful Natures Sheds destructions, which basically means shut down. I guess that's why we're here." She smiled. She had a very confident and kind smile. "Like you, we reside in a deserted bunker, from the pre-catastrophes military days. We learned a lot about how to run the place from Peter and Violet, in terms of maintenance, rosters and all that. There are fewer sanctuaries in the south, so we are limited in the numbers we can liberate, but it doesn't stop us. We still rescue as many as possible. Sometimes we send them all the way around here, if that's the only option." She seemed to have run out of things to say and sat back down. We all clapped excitedly.

Carl indicated he wanted to speak. "Hi everyone. Like Dominique, I want to thank you for the invitation and your warm welcome. Dominique and I are here to share our experience with you, relating to our Natures Farm takeovers, but we are also here to learn from you. I think it's a fantastic opportunity for cells-symbiosis. I think it's a perfect time to have more frequent collaborations between cells. We can see, in the south at least, that there are some exciting changes. Slave farms are closing, people are shifting to ethical life philosophies in droves. For the first time in my life, I think we are truly feeling that total liberation is not just possible, but it's near. Really near. And we must keep fighting for it." The room erupted again into cheers and clapping, some people shouting, "Total Liberation now!"

After a few moments of excited mayhem, Violet stood up again, clapping and thanking our two guests.

"We will start planning our mission tomorrow morning. The following people, please make yourselves available at eight o'clock in the Board Room..." She called out all the names, including mine. And ended with, "Jacqueline, I'd like your presence there too." Roth nodded, and my smile was wiped off my face.

As soon as everyone was invited to enjoy the scrumptious looking cakes and hot tea on the table, I found a moment to grab Violet to the side. "You can't be serious, asking Roth to join us in planning this action."

"I'm dead serious. That farm used to be her kingdom, who better to help us plan this?"

"Don't you think there's a risk she could double cross us?"

"If I thought there was, I wouldn't have asked her there." Violet said, becoming agitated with my interrogation. "Not only does she know the place, but she knows Golf, our secret undercover agent at the farm, better than anyone."

"Roth knows who Golf is? She knows his identity?"

Violet bit her lip, contemplating how to proceed. "Look, Sunny, I know you and Jacqueline had a long and troubled past. But she's been helping us with every mission we have had these past couple of years." I shook my head. In my mind, providing us with some trivial information here and there, did not amount to invaluable help. "She saved your life only a couple of months ago, isn't that a good sign?" I couldn't answer, because indeed *it was* a good sign. "Give her a chance, Sunny." And with that, she excused herself and went mingling in the crowd.

Ben appeared behind me, putting his hand around my waist. "Everything OK?"

"Roth is joining us around the Board Table this time." I said.

"Yes, I heard." He didn't seem happy about it either.

"Violet said Roth knows who Golf is."

"Seriously?"

"Yes. Don't you think it's a risk? Golf is supposed to be this… super-secret silver bullet, being on the inside. If Roth double-crosses us, she can put all of us at risk, including Golf."

Ben nodded. "I don't like it any more than you do."

I lost all interest in cakes and tea, but before Ben and I could sneak out of the Community Room, Carl and Dominique approached us with undeniable excitement.

"You must be Sunny!" Carl said, smiling, the four of us exchanging handshakes. "We've heard so much about you. It's a real pleasure finally meeting you face to face."

"Really? Thank you." I was humbled and surprised. "What have you heard about me?"

"Oh, your escape from Natures is a stuff of legends" Dominique smiled.

"I wasn't alone, and I had lots of help," I said with honesty.

"Your humility is also famous."

Ben hugged me. "She deserves all the compliments," he said proudly, sneaking a kiss to the top of my head. "She's the bravest, most amazing person I've ever met."

All that attention made me cringe. I wanted to leave. "Excuse me, I have a bit of a headache," I apologised to Dominique and Carl. "I'll see you tomorrow at the Board Room. Enjoy your evening."

"What's wrong?" Ben looked worried as we were finally out of the Community Room.

"I just don't like all the Hullaballoo around me," I said. "Makes me feel a bit ill. You can stay if you like."

He smiled, put my hand through his and walked on with me. "I think I know how to get you feeling all better."

He did.

43.

The Board Room was full, with so many names called, proving that overtaking Natures was a big deal. All seats were taken, except for one, saved for Nathan who was compulsively late. It was odd seeing Roth at the table. Having her at the Command Room with Violet during missions was as far as it should have gone. Ben poured us both some water and took my hand in his hand. "I love you" he whispered in my ear. I could feel my cheeks warming.

The room was abuzz with excitement. The atmosphere was somehow different than any other first-meeting Board Room session I'd been to. It was almost as if we had all waited for this one to happen, and now that it finally was, there was a sense of elation in the air.

Finally, Violet walked in, followed by Peter, followed by Nathan not far behind.

"Good morning, everyone. Welcome to mission kick-off." She smiled and made eye contact with everyone. "Our last attempted big mission at Natures Farm didn't go to plan. Our objective back then was to liberate as many as possible, including Sunny and her mother Stella. We all know that while we were successful in rescuing several slaves, including our lovely Pearl…" Pearl smiled, as Miley hugged her briefly, "…all in all, the mission wasn't successful. I also think the objective back then, should have been the destruction of The Shed. But we were following Golf's requests, and as we all know, back then Golf was David, and his main priority was to get Stella out." I could tell everyone was looking at me. Violet continued, "We were able to establish a new Golf at the farm, but we put less emphasis on what Golf says, we also have far less direct contact with Golf now. Still, Golf's involvement in this mission is pivotal. Only Golf can shut down the electric fence from the inside."

"Are we allowed to know who Golf is? In case we see him, we don't want to shoot him." Simon made a good point.

"The confidentiality of Golf's identity is imperative, so I'm sorry, Simon, the answer is no."

Murmurs of disappointment around the table.

"So, we've learned from our mistakes, and we now have some powerful support from our friends in the south," she nodded and smiled to Dominique and Carl, "and from Jacqueline Roth, who we all know used to be a key member of the farm's management. Thank you for joining us, Jacqueline."

There were some polite claps around the table. Roth smiled nodding to Violet.

"In fact, I would like, this time, to ask Jacqueline to give us the introduction to the farm and its routines, from an ex-manager point of view." Violet cleared the stage for Roth to tell us what she knew, or what she remembered about Natures.

"Good morning," Roth smiled, "I must admit that my knowledge of the farm isn't up to date, and a lot of it is still in a haze…" she chuckled, a little uncomfortably. "Erm… where to begin…"

"Tell us about where managers and employees stay on the farm,"

Violet suggested.

"Managers and staff do not reside on the farm. You must also remember that this is just one farm of many that we operate... opera*ted*..." another nervous chuckle. "When we arrive at the farm, we come through the side gate, directly to the Operative building, the one you call The Shed. Operatives are the heart of the farm, the purpose for its existence, its where the milk is produced." She threw me a nervous look.

"What can you tell us about the side gate?"

"It's quite small, in comparison with the main gate. Only managers and staff are allowed through it, not even contractors or visiting staff. We have specially designated electronic keys that open it. It opens only sufficient time for one car to get in and closes itself, automatically. So, each car needs to open it over again, even if you drive up there together."

"Is it well lit?"

"Not as dramatically as the main gate."

"Can you please describe the Operative?"

"There are three ways to access the Operative. The slaves were only allowed in through the main doors, that open towards the living quarters. Managers would use either the side door or the medical door. Both these doors lead to the medical compound. That's where we do most of our exp..." she hesitated, "... experiments." As expected, this word was not well received around the table. "But the medical staff also use this compound to check on the girls if any medical assistance is required. The largest part of the medical compound is Inseminations. That's where we insert semen to the cervix to manipulate pregnancies."

There was a repulsed unrest around the table. "But it's all done very humanely, we don't hurt the girls!" Roth added, only digging herself a deeper hole.

Violet interrupted, "how many workers are on site at any given time?"

"Well, there are normally about five managers and five to ten medical staff during the day, but at night, normally up to two managers and two to five medical staff, maximum. There are also the patrolling women. They're not there on any official capacity, we just found that the girls tend to respond better to them than to us. Their main objective is to scare the slaves from getting close to the fence or to the Operative, but they are powerless, they wouldn't know left from right under pressure."

Pearl and I looked at each other, eyebrows raised. The Patrol Women used to terrify us. We thought they were the most powerful, dangerous people put at the farm to torment us. And now we're told they were only there for show?

"Are all staff armed?"

"Not the medical staff, but the managers are armed. We all carry guns."

"What about the Patrol Guards?"

"The women only carry wooden bats. Most wouldn't use them.

We had to establish them as those scary personas, so we did orchestrate a few beating up sessions for all to see, but the slaves who were beaten were destined for slaughter anyway, and the bashings were very limited, it was the only way to convince the Patrol to do it."

Wow. And to think of all the nights I was cooped up in bed, scared of being beaten to death by the Patrol.

"Tell us about the Operative. The Shed."

"Well, that's where the women are attached to the milkers. The place is quite large. There are seventy-five individual stations that can be occupied and operating in any one time. The women would be brought in, topless, a suction pipe would be attached to each breast, they'd be provided with a nice drug to calm them down, most of them would sleep through the whole thing. It really doesn't hurt them at all. Very gentle."

"Stop with your bullshit!" Pearl's tolerance reached its full capacity.

"Pearl, please." Violet said kindly but firmly. "Jacqueline, just stick to the details, no need to embellish with explanations. Go on."

Roth coughed and continued. "The machines are timed, but there are always a couple of medical staff going around, checking, collecting data, supervising, that kind of stuff.

"Where did you keep all the data?"

"It's part of the medical compound. One of the rooms is just for keeping data on each of our girls. It's how we know they're ripe for insemination, when they've had their periods, body temperature, pregnancy status, and their location, of course."

"Sunny, Pearl, show us your little scars," Violet asked. Pearl and I stretched our arms forward, both showing a small, faint scar close to our wrists. "Those scars are where the electronic chips were indented," Violet explained. "It's where the data about each individual is transmitted from. We will remove and destroy the chips once the liberated slaves arrive at the bunker post-mission. We were told off by the various sanctuaries for not doing that with the slaves we rescued from slaughter a few months ago." She paused, then continued, "Jacqueline, are there any other ways to collect data on the slaves?"

"No."

"Thank you. Does anyone have any other questions for Jacqueline?"

"Yes." Pearl jumped up, "do any of the slaves ever resist? Do any of them ever beg you not to, so-call *inseminate* them?"

"What... I... no... no... it's all very..."

"You're lying!" I jumped to Pearl's aid. "My friends were screaming not to be raped. My best friend killed herself because she didn't want to have a baby!"

"That's... a mistake... I didn't know..."

"Yes, you did. You were there!"

"I can't remember. I'm sorry... I can't remember..."

"Let's take a break!" Violet raised her voice to a near shout. "Sunny, Pearl, come with me please."

Ben squeezed my hand before he let me go and join Pearl outside, where Violet was waiting, looking unimpressed.

"What is the matter with you two? Are you trying to jeopardise this mission?"

"Violet, that woman is full of bullshit!" Pearl was angry.

"She is providing us with information we could only dream of getting! Weren't you listening to her? Half of that stuff we didn't know!"

"What about Golf, I though that's why he's there!" Pearl was not about to let off.

"Do you really think Golf would know half as much as an ex-manager of the farm, Pearl? Besides, we don't have that close a supervision on Golf."

"She's using the stage to clear her name," I tried to explain.

"But no one is buying it. You don't need to jump at her for everyone around the room to know how pathetic her excuses are. But what you're doing is scaring her, putting her on her back foot. We need to make her feel comfortable, so she keeps sharing her knowledge."

"But... doesn't it bother you that she isn't showing any remorse?"

"She does show remorse, Sunny. I know for a fact that she has apologised to you, personally."

"Did you put her up to it? Because I still think it was just an act!"

Violet sighed, impatiently.

Pearl and I exchanged unhappy looks.

"Look, I'm going to be blunt," Violet said, rather angrily, "either you comply, or you're both out of the mission. Am I clear?"

We both nodded.

"Good then, let's get back inside."

44.

"As you heard from Jacqueline Roth, there aren't too many managers and staff present at the farm. This is a huge advantage," Carl said, "which we used when we raided the two farms down south. The element of surprise is critical, though. Because the farms are well connected, security wise, and bringing reinforcements is easy for them."

"Is there a Communications Room at the Operative, Jacqueline?" Violet interrupted him.

"Yes, at the back, not far from the Insemination Room."

"Can you describe it please?"

"Well, there are the closed-circuit monitors. They are very old, from pre-catastrophe days, some aren't working. There are drones, but not as advanced as yours here… I mean *ours*…" she chuckled. "There's an internal comms station where staff can talk to each other, but most medical staff don't wear it. They don't like it. There is a phone that goes directly to the emergency services, and one that goes to sister farms in the area."

Somehow, this sounded a lot less high-techy than what one would expect from a place like Natures.

"Is that it?" Violet seemed to pick up on my thoughts.

"Yes," Jacqueline replied, then added, "the farm… the *industry*… It's way past its heyday…"

"Ok. So, who occupies the Communication Room most of the time?" Violet asked.

"Managers. I used to sit there quite often."

"Thank you. Please, continue, Carl."

Carl nodded. "You seem to have an advantage with your internal person, Golf," he addressed the room. "We didn't have that luxury. So, to my understanding, Golf is in charge of disabling the electric fence?"

"Yes," Violet replied.

"We'll need to know where the disablement point is, for backup. Also, we'll need to come up with a back-up plan, in case Golf doesn't deliver."

"Golf will deliver," Violet replied with confidence.

"Still, we need to know."

"The main power point for the fence is inside the Operative," Jacqueline was quick to respond. On the outer wall of the Communications Room. It needs a special key."

"How many copies do you have of this key?"

"Each manager carries a key on their person. There is also a key inside the Communications Room."

"And Golf has access to the Communications room, Violet?"

"Yes."

"I suggest, then," Carl continued, "that Golf's clear task would not only be to disarm the fence but also to stay guard in place, in case someone tries to enable it again."

Violet nodded.

"Also, does the fence give any sign if the power comes back on?" Carl wondered.

"It takes about a minute to recharge. There should be some flickering red lights at the top of each pole," Jacqueline confirmed.

"OK. Thanks," Carl nodded and continued, "In the case of the farms down south, once the fence was disabled, the gates were automatically opened. Is that the case here too?"

"No," Jacqueline answered. "Disablement of Fence and Gates are independent of each other."

"Is there any other way to open the gates except for an electronic key?"

"No."

"OK, then I guess explosives will be required."

"We divided our main forces into small teams," Dominique picked up from Carl. "It's a strategy we learned from your cell, in fact. But in addition, you will need a large force outside, to help you storm in. These people will be your main raid force, their task focused on evacuating slaves, including children and babies. Do you have a network of volunteers that could do that?"

"The sanctuaries we work with would be able to provide us with quite a few volunteers," Violet confirmed.

"Excellent," Dominique was pleased. "The last thing to remember is, that if you happen to get inside The Shed, or what Jacqueline referred to as the Operative, prepare to be shocked. The smell of the place, the way it's set up, it's quite terrifying. I know you guys were inside slaughterhouses and the likes, but don't underestimate the profound emotional impact this place could have on you."

I couldn't agree more.

Throughout the rest of the day, a plan was formulated, that would see a coordinated attack from several key points, including one at the side gate, south of The Shed. It was time to know who was joining which team.

"I'd like Alpha One to consist of Ben, Pearl, Nathan and Sunny," Violet announced. "And I'd like you, Sunny, to lead."

I was surprised. This would be the first time for me to lead the team. Ben squeezed my hand and smiled, "It's about time, too."

The other teams were announced with their leaders, Leah, Bill and Miley. Almost everyone was involved. Even Phoenix, Simon's partner who rarely joined missions, was named in one of the teams. Command would include Carl and Dominique, and as usual, Venus and Ren would operate the drones.

It was all set. Now we just needed to start practicing.

45.

The mission required a lot of coordination between the teams. We took our time to train and practice, setting the mission date at four months away. A cohort of about one hundred and fifty volunteers was confirmed as our main raiding force, coming from sanctuaries all over the country to help us. They needed to be separately trained, and well controlled. We were expecting them to start arriving during the four weeks prior to the mission. The parking area was converted into a huge camping space, where the volunteers could stay until after the mission, when it would be converted to host the liberated dairy slaves. My friends. My sister.

They started arriving as planned. First in small trickles, then in droves. But having an extra one hundred and fifty people to coordinate over training meant that each session dragged on and on for hours, doing Miley's head in, as the leader of that team.

Jacqueline Roth was again given permission to stand outside with us and observe. It seemed like our team, Alpha One, was her particular interest. I wasn't happy about it but realised by then that complaining wouldn't help.

One balmy evening, as I was making my way back to the room, I spotted Simon and Phoenix hunched together in the Community Room. I wasn't trying to be nosey but couldn't avoid hearing Simon pleading with Phoenix not to participate in the upcoming mission.

"I've had enough staying behind!" Phoenix's soft, yet determined voice wafted thought the door. I continued walking. It was none of my business.

Four months passed in a blink of an eye. After revisiting The Shed in my mind and blowing it up, night after night after night, it was finally time to get out there and do it for real. It was time for me to go back into The Shed.

Sunny's Present Day: Three Years since Joining DaSLiF

46.

I'm ready. My gear is on, my night vision, my gun is loaded. I take a deep breath. Ben and I practiced some yoga in our room before I came down here, to the bus. We both found it was a great way to stretch and breathe before the mission. He's right there with me, his beautiful eyes reassuring me that we're going to be OK. As difficult as it is to believe, by morning, I should have my sister Antim in my custody.

I bend down to retie my shoe. As I stand back up, I'm surprised to see Venus standing right in front of me. But no, I look at her closely and realise, it's actually Ren.

"Brrrrave Sunny," she rolls her R's just like Venus. I think this has to be the first time I hear Ren speak. "I wanted to wish you success in the mission today, I know how important it is to you."

"Thank you, Ren," I smile at her.

"I also wanted to give you something from me," she says to my surprise. She opens her hand to reveal a short flock of her ropey sand-like coloured hair. "A woolly's hair is said to have great protecting qualities. I wish for you to have this, Ms Sunny." She places the hair in my hand. It's ticklish. I give her a little hug, "Thank you Ren. I'll keep it in my pocket."

She smiles and walks away. I really did not expect that at all.

"You have your own fan club," Ben chuckles, and I nudge him with a smile.

Still watching Ren's back disappear inside the bunker, I see Violet coming down the corridor, her steps are quick and deliberate. She's here for me. I can sense it.

"Sunny," she calls me. *Knew it.* "I decided to allow Jacqueline Roth to be part of the mission. On the ground." I can sense my temperature rising. "And I want her to be with your team."

"What? Violet, you can't be serious!"

"I'm very serious. I gave it a lot of thought. Jacqueline is still well recognised at the farm. She can be helpful to you. I'm sure you'll know how to utilise her."

"She should be part of the raiding force, with Miley." I try, knowing it's already hopeless.

"No. She should be with you and your team. I'm confident you'll be able to use her well." Violet says firmly, indicating that this conversation is over. "She's getting ready and should be here soon. Brief her." I still don't know how to respond. "Good luck. You'll be great," she says and disappears back into the bunker.

Ben and I exchange horrified looks. Pearl and Nathan join us, realising something's up.

"We have Roth to babysit," I tell them. They don't seem too pleased. Our comms equipment is already in our ears, meaning, we are live, so we can't say exactly what we think about this. Everything we say is heard and recorded.

And here she comes, the new activist in the flesh. Jacqueline seems extremely proud of herself. "Hi team," she greets us with extra-large smiles. "I'm so happy to be one of your squad!" she says, sounding almost giddy. I can sense the pulse in my neck. I'm not happy about being ambushed like that. I'm not happy with having Roth on the ground, full stop. But it's out of my hands. And it's time to get a move on. For a change, we are not mobilising a bus this time, but one of the black cars. Easier to manoeuvre and hide. Ben is driving and I am riding shotgun. Nathan, Pearl, and Roth are squeezing in the back seat. Nathan and Pearl's faces are sour with the new arrangement, but Roth is as happy as a child on her way to a candy store. *Please don't feel like you need to make conversation the whole way,* I say to myself. She does.

At last, she falls quiet. I guess she could finally sense that no one is keen to talk, except for her. We make our way in silence. I feel every cell in my body tighten. I'm going back to the farm. It is hard to comprehend. I don't think I've ever been this nervous before a mission. Not only am I headed towards the place where my nightmares still reside, but I'm going there with all the extra responsibilities of a team leader. And now I have Roth on my back too. I just can't believe Violet did this to me.

We can see the buses make a turn towards their assembly point, but our car keeps going, through the narrow makeshift roads. We are making our way further, towards the southern side gate. We can't see much, as on both sides overgrown shrubs and hedges block the view. But suddenly, the shrubbery is cleared, as if nature bows in front of Natures, and I can see it right there, to my right. It's the farm. It's The Shed. My stomach twists into a tight knot, and I feel sick.

Ben turns off the lights and the car keeps sliding in darkness, slowly, further towards the gate. He parks it out of sight, hidden behind some wild vegetation, and we disembark. My legs are shaking so badly, I'm afraid I might fall. Ben is right there next to me, "Are you OK, Sunny?"

"Yes, I'm fine." *Get a grip of yourself. You are no longer the child who left this place over three years ago.*

In the boot of the car are five large and heavy gym bags full of explosives. Half a bag is destined to blow open the side gate, everything else – The Shed. We each take a bag, and make our way to the gate, as quietly as possible.

Nathan is our Explosive Master Supreme. He's in charge of wiring the gate. He sets everything out and gets ready. I study Pearl's demeanour. It's a difficult homecoming for her, too. She nods to me. She's fine. The electric fence omits a constant hum. It's alive with powerful electric vitality.

"Alpha One to Omega. We are in Position, over." I think my voice is a little shaky.

One by one all teams confirm their location. Everything is set. Now we're just waiting for the elusive Golf to disconnect the electric fence.

We are crouching as close to the ground as possible, not to be detected by a randomly passing manager or medical staff, or as we used to call them at the farm, White Suits. Nothing happens. The fence is still humming with life. We wait in silence as the clock ticks away.

Where the heck is Golf?

It must be ten minutes already and nothing is happening. The fence is still alive. I'm becoming restless, and so is everyone in the team, including Roth.

"What's happening?" she asks me, trying to keep her voice down, but out here in the open, it sounds like she's shouting.

I don't answer, just shrug. I don't know what's happening.

Just as I wonder if I should contact Omega, someone else does. "Alpha Two to Omega, Fence is still not disconnected, over."

I can hear Violet's voice in my ear, "Wait it out, over." What does it even mean? Just wait and wait until dawn? This mission already frustrates me. We keep waiting. Another ten minutes pass. We look at the fence, and we look at each other, and we look at the fence again, and we look around, until finally, *finally*, we hear a certain 'PLUCK' and the humming stops.

Nathan grabs the special electricity-conducting thingamajig we were provided with, to ensure the fence is indeed dead. He tosses it at the fence. Nothing happens, except it makes a dull thud as it falls to the ground. That's it, all systems go. We run to the fence. Nathan slowly and carefully picks up the portion of the explosives allocated for blowing up the side gate. He places it strategically, vertically along the gate line on both the stationary and the sliding elements. His fingers move fast as he wires each piece and connects it all together.

"We're all set," he whispers. "Take a few steps back!"

"Alpha One, we are Go," I let my peers know that we're ready with our explosives. All teams must switch their explosives in unison. We wait for the other two teams to confirm status.

"Alpha Two, we are Go," Leah's confirmation from her position at the front gate, follows ours soon after.

As we wait for Alpha Three, I sense something is changing around us. Something is off. There is a sense, as if... there is a hum... I watch the poles. A red light is flickering. The fence is recharging back on!

"Alpha Three..." Bill's voice comes through the comms, as I can hear myself screaming "THE FENCE IS ALIVE!! TAKE COVER!"

There are a few split seconds of complete panic, then we spread ourselves flat on the ground, covering our faces. The fence makes a "PLUCK" and where explosives were attached, there is a wild BANG! And a huge lightning feast of bolts and fire shoots burning rockets everywhere. I can hear Nathan yelling. His leg is on fire. I push myself towards him and pat it out as quickly as possible.

In the comms there are screams. Loud, semi-hysterical screams, "ALPHA THREE TO OMEGA, WE HAVE A FATALITY! I REPEAT, WE HAVE A FATALITY!" *No! That should NOT have happened!* "It's Phoenix. Omega, do you copy?"

"We copy, Alpha Three."

I'm expecting some more instructions, what to do? Phoenix is lost! Are we supposed to continue as we are? HOW? Nothing else comes through the comms. I can feel my heart. It's about to explode.

"Shit man, what happened?" Nathan shouts, not even making the slightest effort to maintain silence. There's no point with this firework display we've just put on.

"Golf fucked up," Ben says.

I look at the fence. The fire and lightning are reduced. I can see that there is a gap that we can run through. Would we get fried if we did?

"We can run through that gap in the gate!" I suggest.

"This is not a suicide mission," Ben replies. "We should abort. All of us, we need to abort mission."

No. No. No. I did not come all this way, back to the farm, so close, to abort. No way.

I get myself a little closer to the gate. The gap is very tempting to run through. *Don't be insane.* I search my brain, what should I be doing? When suddenly, just like that, "PLUCK" and the humming is out again. Like a sick little game, the fence is dead again, but for the small residue of lightning.

"INSIDE! NOW!" I yell at my team.

We run inside with everything we've got. Nathan limping on his hurt leg. We've lost so much precious time, there is no way we could still disable the three white cars in the small staff parking.

"Ben, Nathan, Pearl, continue into the shed, blow the damn thing up!" I order, handing Ben the explosives bag I'm carrying. He grabs it, they nod and move towards the imposing building.

"YOU!" I grab Roth by her shirt and drag her behind me as I run into the medical ward. I remember this place so well. The Natures propaganda posters are still on the wall, with their crumpled edges and fading colours. I smash the door that leads deeper inside with my boot.

"Where are we going?" Roth asks, panting, as I still clutch her shirt with my fist.

"We're going to get to the power unit that charges the fence, and YOU are going to guard it with your life! No one turns it back on! Do you understand?"

She nods, with the limited neck movement my clutching allows.

I run inside. I'm now in the room where, years ago, I saw, for the first time, all my dead brothers floating in sickening jars. It was then that I realised my mother had many more pregnancies and births than I thought. And here I am again, the jars are still there, and there are more of them. So many more. Babies of all sizes, floating in yellowish liquid inside jars. But I'm not afraid of it anymore. In fact, to my utter surprise, I feel nothing. Nothing at all. I just need to get to the power unit. The fence mustn't recharge, no matter what.

I kick the next door down. One more room and we're aligned with the 'Operative'. Big glass windows separate the medical ward, where I am, and The Shed. I can already smell the pungent smell of sour breastmilk and urine. I can see the sickly green on the walls inside. Ben, Nathan, and Pearl will be inside there soon, blowing it sky high. Nathan must be wiring the entrance doors right now. I turn my head briefly, just to take in the full sight of this abhorrent place, when my mouth opens in horror. There are about twenty armed

White Suits inside. Waiting.

I drop low to the floor, taking Roth down with me, not sure if we were seen through the windows or not.

"Alpha One, twenty armed inside. I repeat twenty armed inside!"

"Roger that," Ben confirms.

"What's going on?" Roth asks.

"We've been anticipated!" I respond, when suddenly, I'm filled with a deep, heavy, poignant suspicion. "How did they know we were coming, Roth?" I ask her. There's rage and bitterness in my voice.

"I… I don't know!"

"Really? Don't you?"

"Nnnn…no."

I grab my gun, and she shrinks back, quivering. I wasn't planning to shoot her, only to protect us both, in case we were seen. But her reaction makes me wish I could. Oh, how I wish I could. But I'm not that kind of person. I wouldn't and I don't. Instead, I grab her again and, as low as possible, I move forward, deeper in, towards the communications room.

We pass through the insemination hall. This is where my escape began. I watched my friends being raped, and I knew I couldn't stay there. My mother ordered me to run, and so I did. The place makes the hair on my skin stand on end.

I don't even manage to pass all the way through, when a White Suit jumps at me from behind the closed curtains of a cubicle. My hand releases Roth, who is quick to run out of there. The White Suit fires his gun. He misses me by a mile and tries again. *I'm not afraid of you!* I leap at him and swing him straight into a choking position. My arms tighten around his neck. He wriggles and pushes, cackling with the lack of oxygen. He manages to release himself, but before he decides what to do next, I shoot his left foot. He drops screaming to the floor. I grab his gun and run out.

Where the heck is Roth?

I keep running in, not long now is the Communication Room. I find Roth crouched on the floor, leaning against the wall across from the room. She's signalling to me. Showing me two fingers, then pointing to the door of the Communication Room. I'm guessing that means there are two White Suits inside. Crouching all the way to the door I take a quick peep inside the Communication Room. My attempt to see what's inside is answered by five shots fired at the door. I could vaguely trace the location of the two occupants of the room. There's no option but to go in with guns blazing. Luckily, I now have two. I draw and aim as precisely as I can, and I run inside immediately taking cover behind the nearest desk. One of my shots hit one of the White Suits, seems like I got him in the knee. He's screaming in pain, grabbing his leg rocking himself on his back, side to side. I rise up from behind the desk, shooting blindly at the direction of the other White Suit. I'm met with a shot coming my way. It grazes my arm. I drop to the floor, my arm set on fire. I bite my lips and groan with pain. The burning sensation temporarily paralyses me from top to bottom. I can feel I'm bleeding, but I can still make use of my arm. I need to get better access to the White

Suit. There is the communications bay, located not far from me to the right. If I can run to it and take cover, I could angle my shots better towards the White Suit. My first attempt at jumping over from behind the desk is met with another near hit by the White Suit. *Darn, this guy is good with his gun!* I take my chance again, leaping towards the Communication Bay. His shot misses me by an inch and hits the bay, just as I manage to shield behind it. *This is going to be a long night.* I briefly emerge up from behind the bay, taking my best aim at the White Suit. He's hiding and I miss. *Shit.* I'm thinking what to do next, when suddenly I hear Roth speak.

"Dr Croydon, what do you think you're doing?"

There's some shuffling from behind the Communications Bay. "Dr Roth? Is that you?"

"Yes, of course it's me. Why are you shooting?"

"There are terrorists here. Shooting." He says, his voice rather shaky for someone who aims so well.

"What are you talking about? What terrorists?"

He stands up. "There are…" but I don't wait for him to finish his sentence, I jump to my feet, and I shoot him in his thigh. He falls to the floor, screaming.

I look at Roth. Did she actually devise this cunning attempt to give me a break? I find that hard to believe somehow, but planned or not, she helped me overcome my opponent. I nod to her. "Good job. Now, show me where the fence control box is."

She leads me out. I can hear a cacophony of firearms shooting inside The Shed. It's a full-on battle. I need to get myself in there, to help my friends out.

"There it is!" Roth point at the box. The key is inside, it is switched to 'off'.

"Roth, you stay here and guard this box. No one touches it. No one."

I turn to leave as she asks, "don't I get to have a gun?"

I hesitate. In my mind I can see her grabbing the gun, pointing it at me and shooting me. "No. Anyone comes you call me via comms," I say and run back towards the internal doors to The Shed. As I get to the internal glass windows I crouch and take a brief look. Inside I can see Ben and Pearl taking cover behind two islands of milking stations. Nathan is busy wiring the Island where Ben is. Six White Suits are lying on the floor, injured.

I smash my way through the doors, catching the White Suits with their backs to me, by complete surprise. I manage to hit four of them as I run to take cover behind a milking station. I can feel the menacing cold metal of the station against my body, and it sends chills through my spine. The machine, towering above me, is dormant now. Its greedy breastmilk sucking cups are lying limp at the end of its still long and twisted tentacles. *No more breastmilk is going to be stolen by these abhorrent devices. Not if I can help it.* A brief, sordid vision of my mother being forcefully hooked up to one of these stations goes through my mind. *How many times was she exploited this way? How could she tolerate this abuse?* I shake away these thoughts to the sound of bullets bouncing around me in a tirade of attempts to kill me. These

White Suits weren't aiming at the legs, they wanted the head. I fire into the room, making sure not to aim anywhere near Ben and Pearl. I hit a couple more. Ben and Pearl hit a few as well. I feel the burn in my arm intensify. I need to bandage my wound. I peep from behind the milking machine to reassess the room. I'm surprised to see there's a White Suit hiding very close to me. I aim to shoot when I see, as clear as day, that he had just wet himself. *He's scared.* Against my better judgement, I feel sorry for him. In his mind he's probably an innocent employee, just doing his job. Maybe someone had put a gun in his hand and told him to defend this 'Operative'. He turns his head back and spots me. He raises his hands up. I can see his mouth trembling. "Throw me your weapon," I order him. He takes his gun and tosses it my way, on the floor. I nod to him. He's safe. "Cover me, I'm moving to Pearl's site" Nathan says, already in motion. Only five more White Suits are still functioning in the room. I take one down, Ben takes two more.   Nathan is wiring away, when a White Suit takes a direct aim at him, hitting Pearl in the shoulder. "SON OF A BIIIIITCH!" She screams in pain. Something in the way she screams makes me jump out from behind my cover, shooting like mad. I hit the last two White Suits.

I rush to Pearl as Ben moves between the injured White Suits, takes their weapons, and ties them up. The one White Suit who surrendered to me earlier, offers his hands willingly. Pearl is bleeding profusely. "I need to get you out of here," I say.

"Nathan what's our status?" I ask him.

"We're almost done," He says, "Four minutes max." I can't wait to see this place blowing sky high.

"Ben, hurl the White Suits out, we don't want to set this place alight when there are people in here."

Ben starts hassling the White Suits, limping, and hopping, groaning, and moaning, out and away from The Shed. Some resist, only to be told that the place is about to be blown to smithereens in a couple of minutes. They all find the strength to carry themselves out afterwards. I put my arm under Pearl and help her to her feet. She leans all her weight on me, wincing and struggling with her pain. We make our way, stumbling out. I'm shocked to see the place. It's a war zone. Apparently, armed White Suits were hiding all over the place. All our teams were engaged in fighting. I canvas the grounds. Most White Suits were already disarmed. Some activists were lying on the ground, nursing various injuries. Volunteers were rushing around, attempting to get people out. Ben returns to me after ensuring all White Suits were out of danger of our looming explosives. "Ben, take Pearl out of here. I need to evacuate the White Suits from the Comms Room and get Roth out."

"She double-crossed us, Sunny. They were prepared for us. They knew we were coming."

"I'm not going to leave her here to explode," I say as I transfer Pearl's aching body to be carried by Ben. Slowly, they start to make their way out towards the main gate.

"What's the status, Nathan?"

"One minute."

I run back inside The Shed. The place is completely smeared with fresh blood. Nathan is still busy laying down wires. I make my way towards the internal door. The large glass window is completely shattered on the floor. I turn and run towards the Communications Room. My heart stops. *Where's Roth?* "Roth? ROTH? JACQUELINE ROTH?" I call to her, but she's gone. I look inside the Communications room, it's empty. There's no one to evacuate. I check the fence control box. It's still set to "Off". In less than a minute this box would be out of reach anyway. The key is still inside. I grab it and start running, making my way out. "Roth?" I call into the insemination hall. She's not there.

"Thirty Seconds"

"Roth is gone."

"The sneaky double-crossing witch!" I hear Ben spitting what I was already thinking.

"Get out, Sunny!" Nathan is calling me with urgency.

"Ten Seconds!" Nathan keeps the clock ticking.

I'm running as fast as I can, my arm is throbbing. I burst out of the doors, I'm out. I keep running, my head is turned back, completely missing the fact that there is someone in my way. "Sunny!" I turn my head around and I'm met with the full force of a heel of a gun. The world spins, I can feel my body smashing to the ground, and then everything turns black.

47.

Everything is a haze of dust, and heat, and fire. My ears are ringing so badly, I can hear nothing but thunderclaps inside my head. My head… it's splitting with pain. I can feel blood trickling into my left eye. Through the cotton balls that my ears seem to be filled with, I think I can hear someone screaming my name. "Sunny! Sunny!"

I look up, everything is so blurry and dim, like the lights in my brain were turned off. Someone is standing above me. There's a gun pointing to my head.

"Roth?" I can hear myself mumbling. Or maybe I'm just imagining myself mumbling because I'm not sure I actually say anything. The gun hovers above my head. I close my eyes. I was born in this shitty place, I guess I'm going to die here too. Roth won, in the end. Not everything in life is fair. I'm waiting. Nothing is happening. No shot is fired. When I open my eyes, I can see a figure walking away, slightly limping. Ben skids to my side, "Sunny!"

"Ben…"

He helps me up and supports me. "You were too close to the explosion. Why didn't you run further?"

I can barely speak. "I was ambushed."

"You were right about her from the start. We should all have listened to you!" He's angry. I nod. I can't speak. Everything is so strange. I feel like I just woke up from a weird and twisted dream.

He's leading me towards the main gate. I look around. The building where I spent all my childhood, together with my best friend Rosy Cheeks is ablaze, as are the other buildings. "We've got everyone out," Ben tells me. "Come, there's someone very special you need to see."

I know who he means, and I'm overwhelmed with joy.

We walk out through the main gate. This will be the last time I leave this bloody place. Ben helps me onto the bus. I see her immediately. She's so pretty! The spitting image of Stella. She sits there, covered in a blanket, her big blue eyes searching the bus.

I walk to her. I can already feel my tears rolling, "Antim," I whisper, my voice breaking.

"Are you Sunny?" she asks, in her sweet voice.

"Yes!" I cry and hug her; my tears are now proper sobs.

I kiss her head and pet her cheeks. "You look so much like our mother," I say.

"Where is she?" Antim asks, her big eyes staring at me, full of question.

"They haven't told you?" I gasp in shock, "Oh sweetheart, she died. I'm so sorry. Someone should have told you."

She leans her head against my chest, and I hug her. My heart is so overflowing with happiness, I can't even feel my burning arm anymore.

The bus is moving. I look outside the window and to my delight, I see The Shed is engulfed in flames, its roof collapsed, the walls destroyed. This Natures Farm is no more.

*

I keep hugging Antim all the way to the bunker. I'm sliding in and out of troubled sleep myself. I can't shake the feeling that something is off. There's a fog I'm desperately trying to clear, without success.

We're the second bus to reach the bunker. The large parking space is full of both volunteers and liberated slaves. All wrists of the newly rescued women, girls and babies are being methodically de-chipped. I'm sure if I walk around, I'll meet so many women I've known all my life, but I need to get Antim medically checked, and I need to sort out my wounded head and arm. Someone is calling me, but I decide to ignore it. There will be enough time for social reunions in the days to come.

On my way to the Medical Ward, I see Bill, George and Simon hunched around a dining table, all smeared in blood and extremely distraught. Simon is sobbing. George notices me and makes eye contact. Tears sting my eyes. Phoenix is gone. He's gone. We weren't very close, but we were colleagues and I liked him. I'm overcome with grief. Phoenix is our first death. Everyone will be deeply impacted by this. "I'm so sorry," I whisper. George nods.

I steer Antim towards the Medical Ward. It is bustling with activity. Most liberated women are in fine shape. Our volunteers did a stellar job making sure no one got hurt. Those currently pregnant are checked and let back in the converted parking lot. The occupied beds are mostly taken with wounded activists. I see Jessica with a bleeding leg, Suzy's face is hurriedly bandaged, Pearl is being pushed into surgery. Billie notices my bleeding face and arm. "Sunny, come, lie down on this bed, here," she points out a bed near where I stand.

"Can you please examine my sister, first? I need to know she's OK."

Billie smiles. "So, you're the famous Antim, then?" she asks the girl. Antim nods.

Billie calls out a volunteer and asks her to ensure Antim is checked. "Make sure she's de-chipped," she instructs the volunteer. Antim and the volunteer leave, and Billie gently but firmly ushers me onto the bed. I try to hop on, but it feels more like collapsing into it. As usual, I don't appreciate the severity of my injuries until I'm put on a medical bed. I feel the world twirling around me.

Billie checks my injured head. There's a buzz in my ears. "A bandage would do the job on this one, but you are probably heavily concussed." She then pulls a pair of shears and cuts my shirt off to examine my arm. "It's deep. You need stitches. But you were very lucky my dear, very lucky indeed."

"It's the hair."

"The what?"

"The hair. Ren's hair."

Billie smiles without the foggiest idea what I'm talking about.

"Is Ben here?" I ask her.

"I'll make sure to send him right in when he arrives," she

promises as the big needle with the Sleeping Gift enters my skin.

I want to say something else. It's on the tip of my tongue. I want to say something about the fog, but it's too late. My tongue is heavy and I'm off to Sleepy Land.

48.

I'm dreaming. It's one of those dreams... even in my sleep I just know it's one of those. I'm on the ground outside of the bombed up shed. My ears are drumming and there is a heavy haze all around me. I'm trying to see what's going on. Someone is pointing a gun at me. Why? Why am I not shot at? I try to see but there is a thick layer of fog. There's something I need to hear. I just sense it. I'm trying to sharpen my perception. Through the cotton balls in my head, I finally manage to grasp onto a thread. I hold on to it until finally, I can hear something. A trace of a noise. I concentrate on it. Someone is calling my name. No... they're actually screaming my name, hysterically "SUNNY! SUNNY! HELP ME! SUNNY HELP! HELP ME!"

I turn my head. Who is it? I can see someone in the distance. They're struggling. They're being pushed, shoved into a car. Who is it? I look, I really look, with everything that my dream allows me, I fight to clear the fog away. The person is shoved into the car, struggling, calling me, crying for help. It's... it's... it's...

"Roth?" I can hear myself mumbling. Or maybe I'm just imagining myself mumbling because I'm not sure I actually say anything. The gun hovers above my head. I close my eyes. I'm ready to die. This is where I die. No. Don't close your eyes. Open them. OPEN! I obey my dream and I open my eyes. Someone is there, holding the gun. "Golf? Is this you?" I stare. With all the strength the dream allows me to have, I stare. Something in this person is familiar. Very familiar. I see the barrel of the gun pointing at my head. My eyes follow it to up towards the hand that holds the gun, up towards the arm, up towards the shoulder, up to the neck, I can see... the face... I can see... THE FACE! I... I... *No!* It's impossible! NOOOOOO!

The gun fires.

I awake.

49.

My heart is beating so fast, I can barely catch my breath. I feel the cold sweat on my back. I know who Golf is! *I know who Golf is!*

Ben jumps up from the cushioned chair at my bedside. "What are you doing, Sunny?" he asks in complete horror, as I rip the IV line out of my hand, pressing the entry point to stop the bleeding. Hurriedly, I tie a loose bandage around it as I jump out of my bed. "Sunny? What are you doing?" Ben asks again, he's at a complete loss.

"I know who Golf is!" I say, my voice trembling, my entire body shaking.

"Have you lost your mind? You're wounded, Sunny, can't this wait?"

"I certainly haven't lost my mind. I need to speak to Violet. Now."

"What?"

"Roth didn't double cross us, Ben."

"What? What are you talking about?"

"It wasn't Roth. Roth didn't double cross us. It wasn't her. I was wrong!"

I start running towards the Command Room. Regardless of the late hour, Violet is sure to be there, with the fuckup with a capital F that just happened with this mission, with Golf, with Phoenix dying, with the ambush we walked into.

Ben is right behind me. In spite of my injuries and general state, I'm fast with the rush of adrenaline.

I barge into the Command Room. I must be a sight with my bandage to my head, the arm wound and the makeshift IV Line bandage.

"Sunny?" Violet calls surprised. I can tell by the way her makeup is smudged under her eyes that she is distressed.

I push her out of my way, as I walk straight to the controls, to bring up the archive.

"Sunny, what are you doing?" Venus asks.

"Out of my way, please Venus." I say firmly. She pushes herself away from the controls.

I sift through the archived files with such a rush to my head, I can barely see what I'm looking at.

"Sunny, what…" Violet starts but I raise my hand sharply to silence her.

There! I found it. I bring it up and I press play. It's a night view. The screen is alight with bright green. The people can be seen very clearly. Two of them. They're running. A man and a woman. And here they are, stopping. Turning around. Here is Roth holding a gun, and there's a White Suit man next to her, he's also holding a gun. The man and the woman exchange some words. The guns fire. They fall to the ground. The screen turns to black. I rewind the recording. The guns fire. They fall to the ground. Black. I rewind the recording again. The guns fire. They fall to the ground. How have I missed this? I've watched this recording so many times. How did I not SEE?

"Sunny…" Violet starts, but I am not in the mood.

"Who is Golf, Violet?"

"Sunny…"

"WHO IS GOLF, VIOLET?"

"I…"

I smack my hand on the desk so hard, everyone jumps. "WHO. IS. GOLF. VIOLET?"

"I think you already know, Sunny…" she whispers.

"I want YOU to say it!" I can feel the tears coming down my cheeks again.

She looks at me, her eyes are also filled with tears.

"SAY IT! SAY IT GODDAMIT SAY IT! WHO IS GOLF?"

Violet takes a deep sigh.

"It's Stella," she says finally, her voice a little croaky. "Stella is Golf."

I feel my knees buckle as I fall to the floor, shaking, howling with uncontrollable sobs.

50.

Ben helps me to a chair. His face is frozen in a shocked expression. *He didn't know.* Well, at least that's a relief. He holds my hand, looking accusatively at Violet. She is silent, standing shamefaced, biting her lips. I let the sobs die down and wipe my face.

"What gave it away?" she asks me finally, which angers me even more. No apology, no explanation, she just wants to know how I found out.

"I saw her. At the farm. She was going to kill me."

Violet closes her eyes temporarily and presses them with her fingers.

"My own mother was pointing a gun to my head, staring at me. She was going to *kill* me!"

Violet looks at Peter, Peter looks at Violet. They are both equally guilty of deceiving me. Of deceiving all of us.

"But if you really want to know what in the recording gave it away, it's the angle of the gun. The gun pointing to David was aimed at his chest. Roth is aiming lower. She probably hit Stella in the knee. It explains the slight limp. She never meant to kill her, did she?"

"No," Violet whispers. "No. They had other plans for her."

"I think we need some explanations," Ben says, he still looks completely dumbfounded.

Violet nods her head. She takes a seat, facing me.

"They captured your mother that night. They were planning to turn her for a long time."

"What's with everyone *turning* everyone else? Is this a game to you?" I say with frustration.

"These people, they don't do it like us. We use benign methods. Encouragement. Education. Persuasion. We don't manipulate the brain with drugs and chemicals like them. Their methods are much more powerful. I've never heard of someone who was turned by them and could be turned back, but with your mother, from the beginning, it was different. I believe it's her deep and profound love for you, for Antim and David that kept the real Stella in there, somewhere. She wasn't fully turned. It's unheard of. It shows how strong she was... is... It was she who contacted us and suggested she'd assume the role of Golf, in effect becoming a double agent."

It's so hard to follow. My head is pulsing.

"What did they make her do?"

Violet takes a deep breath. "To all means and purposes, she was turned into a White Suit. Jacqueline Roth trained her herself. But she was resilient. Always empathetic. She was never fully one of them."

"How do you know all that?"

"Because Jacqueline Roth told us."

I shake my head. "She remembered that?"

Violet smiles a faint little smile. "Jacqueline Roth remembered everything."

"WHAT?"

"She didn't have a memory loss."

I grab my head in my hands. Was I going insane? How many lies?

"Sunny, Jacqueline Roth was fully turned. She became one of us. She did not double cross us. She never meant to. She was repentant. She wanted to make up for what she's done, especially to you. We knew that the only way to help you forgive her and give her a chance was if you thought she couldn't remember."

"And now they have her!" I shout. So many lies. So. Many. Lies.

Violet nods, her eyes are glistening with tears.

I can't believe this. I've been played for so long. How dumb am I?

"So why did Stella double cross us? What happened? You say she was a double agent, why did she betray us?"

"I guess they kept working on her, trying to erase the old Stella. We didn't know. I guess they almost succeeded."

"Almost? ALMOST? Phoenix is dead! What kind of 'almost' is that?"

"She didn't kill you. She recognised you and she hesitated. She let you live. Somewhere inside of her there's still the old Stella."

Tears come rolling down my face again. "Can we bring her back?"

"That's never been done. I've never seen anyone recover from being turned."

I let my tears wash my cheeks. My hands are shaking.

"I don't understand," Ben is pacing around, his agitated hand in his hair, "How could you have trusted her? You sent us in there, knowing full well that she might not be all there. You KNEW that shit could happen, and still you let us go in there?"

"I didn't realise how bad it was. It was my mistake. It'd become clear when she hesitated with the fence, turning it off and on and off again…" There are tears in Violet's eyes now. Her voice is frail. "She could have brought an entire army to meet you, instead there were only a few armed medical staff and managers. These were no fighters. It shows you that she's still conflicted, even now."

Ben is furious. "No fighters? You care telling it to Pearl who is still in surgery? Or to Suzy? Or Jessica? Or Sunny?" He came to stand beside me, his hand on my shoulder.

"The mission was successful, Ben. The Shed was destroyed. The Farm is gone…" Violet's voice trembles.

"Successful…. Why don't you ask Simon if he thinks the mission was successful?"

"Phoenix knew the risks. You all knew the risks."

"But we didn't know that our lives were dependent on a messed up double agent with some serious loyalty issues! You lied to us, and you kept lying to us and you're still lying to us." Ben's voice is shaking. He is fuming.

Violet nods her head. "I'm sorry."

I look at her. I'm at a loss. What do I do now? How do I go on from here? I spent almost three years suspecting a woman who had only clear intentions towards me, while the only person who continually lied to me was the woman I trusted above all others. The one I looked up to. I never thought anyone could break my trust so completely.

I feel faint. My head is spinning and there's a ringing in my ears. Ben catches me as I'm about to fall to the floor. "I'm taking you back to the Medical Ward, Sunny." He helps me up to my feet. I lean on him as we make our way out of the room. I look back at Violet once more. She looks as broken as my heart feels.

EPILOGUE

FOUR WEEKS LATER

Sunny paces through the large, airy living room of the beach house. Her two sisters, Spirit, and Antim, run to her for hugs and kisses. She obliges with pleasure. Once greetings are over and done with, the girls run off, playfully chasing each other, filling the house with their childish giggles. Sunny smiles. She knew Rose and Jonathan would adopt Antim in a heartbeat, and Spirit is elated with the presence of a younger sister. Antim follows her around like a shadow, and Spirit could not be happier.

Sunny pauses, looking straight on, through the large sliding glass doors that lead outside to the deck and further, the beach. The woman she came to see is standing there, on the beach, her back is turned to the house, her eyes transfixed with the perpetual crush of the angry waves.

Slowly, Sunny slides the doors open and steps out to the deck. The salty, fresh breeze caresses her face gently. She takes a deep breath. She has always found this place therapeutic. She takes the two steps down onto the beach. The woman, still with her back turned, is wearing a plain, light blue shirt and wide grey pants. Her long brown hair is loose, lightly tussled by the soft wind, her bare feet are planted firmly in the sand. Sunny walks towards the woman, who can clearly sense her presence now, though still not turning around. Sunny reaches the woman. They both stand side by side, facing the sea.

"Hello Violet," Sunny says cordially.

"Sunny." The woman replies.

"How have you been?"

"I'm fine," Violet answers.

Sunny nods. "That's good."

An uncomfortable silence follows. The crush of the waves fills the air with small droplets. Sunny allows the meditative, repeated bounce of the waves onto the shore to instil a sense of calmness in her.

"We've traced Roth," Sunny breaks the silence. "We're planning a mission to get her back into our custody."

"That's good news," Violet says.

Sunny nods.

"What else is new at the bunker?" Violet asks suddenly, her gaze still focused on the sea.

"Phoenix had his funeral. We all went. It was a beautiful ceremony," Sunny says. There's a deep sadness in her voice. "After that, Simon left. Well, technically he's just taking a break, but we think he's probably not coming back."

Violet listens but says nothing.

"Dawn, my old friend from Natures Farm, joined us after the rescue. She miscarried two pregnancies since the day I escaped the farm. They would've certainly sent her to slaughter if it happened again. She's already doing really well with her training." Sunny pauses. She closes her eyes, sensing the rhythm of the sea. "Peter is leaving."

Violet gasps a tiny, near-silent gasp, but Sunny could still hear it.

"He said he's going to go back south at the end of next month. That's when Carl and Dominique were supposed to leave, to return to their home cell, but since then they both decided to stay with us, so Peter might be departing sooner."

Violet bows her head, staring at her feet, burying her toes deeper in the sand.

Sunny turns to face the other woman. "When are you coming back to DaSLiF, Violet?" Her voice is kind.

"You want me back?" Violet asks in undisguised surprise, finally turning to face Sunny.

"I think I've finally learned something from my experience with Roth," Sunny says.

"Learned what?" Violet wonders.

"Forgiveness."

Violet smiles. She takes Sunny in. "Look at you, Sunny. You are a woman now. So much like your mother. Strong, beautiful, tough… a real leader."

Sunny feels her cheeks warming, but she says nothing.

"I'm not coming back, Sunny." Violet says, finally.

"Why?" Sunny is clearly taken by surprise.

"I've made too many mistakes. Especially with you. I should have been so much more open with you. I shouldn't have denied you the truth. I should have listened to you more… and Phoenix… it's totally my fault."

Sunny draws her breath to say something, but Violet cuts her off. "It is time for me to step down. I'm Old Guard. DaSLiF needs new leaders. New vision. New fighters. DaSLiF needs *you*, Sunny. You need to lead it now."

"Violet, I…"

"Ben will be there to help you, and so will Pearl and Nathan. People look up to you, Sunny, and you don't even know it, but they do. You lead, they will follow." She looks at Sunny kindly.

"What will you do?" Sunny wonders.

"Oh, I don't know. I thought I might relocate north. Maybe help out with The Lost Boys. It's been a while since I've seen Bella."

Sunny's eyebrows shoot up in surprise. "You've met her?"

Violet laughs, "I did. She's incredible, isn't she?"

Sunny chuckles, "She sure is!"

The two women laugh. All tension is broken. The atmosphere is comfortable and forgiving. They hug warmly, and Sunny turns to leave. As she takes the two steps back onto the deck, Sunny remembers that just over three years ago, this exact spot is where Violet recruited her to join DaSLIF.

Things have changed so much since then. But the world hasn't changed quite enough. The industries of exploitation, abuse, torture, and death are still out there. They are collapsing, yes. One by one they are being brought down by dedicated activists like her and her friends. But the work isn't done yet. Sunny was determined to make sure that it was. And if she needs to lead, then so be it. Total liberation was coming, and the world had better watch out.

This book is a work of fiction… Or is it?

Find out here:

www.watchdominion.com

The End